# Perfection
## By
## Jeffery Martin Botzenhart

ALL RIGHTS RESERVED

Publisher's Note:

This is a work of fiction. All names, characters, places, and
events are the work of the author's imagination.

Any resemblance to real persons, places, or events is
coincidental.

Solstice Publishing - www.solsticepublishing.com

# Part One
## Deception

# Chapter One

Breathing heavy as if just having run a marathon, Piers glanced worriedly down both directions of the brightly lit hallway. He felt certain he was being watched. Surveillance and cell phone cameras were forbidden in this part of the tower due to nature of the secretive work being accomplished in his division. One concept he'd learned in his years of devotion to Tyco Innovations repeated in his mind. *Someone is always watching.* A career spent under a constant corporate spyglass fostered his rampant paranoia. A moment's relief from his anxiety eased his suspicious nature when the elevator doors opened.

"Parking Deck B," he urged through voice command. The elevator doors closed silently.

After checking the time on his vintage silver pocket watch, Piers sighed as he then looked at his faint reflection on the window of the glass elevator. His haggard appearance matched the fatigue he felt from a week of mostly sleepless nights. Beyond his image, glimmering lights from the towers of downtown Chicago corrupted the January darkness. At a quarter past nine, most of these offices were empty of their employees hours ago. The tower always remained lit to convey a brilliant lie to deceive people into thinking a vibrant workforce continued laboring late amidst this corporate realm.

He glanced up when noticing the flicker of the overhead light. He felt no hesitation with the elevator's decent but was mildly concerned about this. After a few more flickers, the interior plunged to darkness. Looking outside, he expected the city lights to grow brighter, yet they appeared translucent, as if blocked by something he couldn't see.

Reminded of flashes of lightning, the elevator light returned. Piers exhaled his relief, though troubling thoughts regarding the momentary failure lingered. Being a friend of the world-famous architect, who designed this tower, all had been well planned, using the most efficient and technologically advanced components to construct this eighty-two story steel and glass wonder. She would be appalled to learn that a cheap light bulb had been installed in the main corporate elevator.

"Good evening, Doctor Hylant," a synthetic, yet pleasant male voice greeted, startling Piers.

"Good evening, Darwin," he responded, huffing lightly. Carrying on a conversation with the voice of a sophisticated supercomputer was the last thing he wanted to do tonight.

"I have called for a company car to be waiting for you at parking deck A," Darwin continued over the hum of the descending elevator.

"I prefer to drive my own car home tonight," Piers said while rubbing his irritated eyes.

"The weather forecast is for heavy snowfall in the Chicago area, which began an hour ago. From your personal health monitor on your left wrist, I have detected high levels of stress, an accelerated heartbeat and pulse, and strained vision. If you would like, Doctor Hylant, I could continue with a detailed health diagnostic for you?"

Piers again observed his fifty-seven year old reflection in the windowed wall opposite where he stood in the elevator. His grey hair and five o'clock shadow of whiskers made him look more like sixty-seven. His frumpy frame and the fatigue from a long day added to this. Sighing, he thought, *I wasted my youth in this horrible place, too many times led my morons in being forced to strive for the unobtainable. No one can achieve perfection. We're all too damn human.*

"No," Piers rejected this. "I'm feeling fine. It was just a long day."

"There are twenty-four hours in a day," Darwin confirmed. "All days are equal in hours."

"It was...oh, never mind," Piers grumbled, growing irritated by this conversation. "Please call for my own car to be waiting for me."

"I apologize, Doctor Hylant, but I am unable to fulfill this request. Corporate health protocols must be followed to perfection when considerations for the safety of Tyco Innovations employees are addressed."

"Son-of-a-bitch," Piers uttered in disgust under his breath. "Fine, have it your way," he mumbled, closing his eyes. *If I want to go home, this is the only way that stupid piece of shit will let me leave.*

The elevator came to a gentle halt. A burst of cold wind greeted Piers as the doors opened. Chilled by the brisk air gusting through the parking deck, his body trembled as he waited for the company car to arrive. Seeing it approach, he breathed out his relief. The door of a sleek, jet-black electric car opened like the rising wing of a bird. Once seated, he secured his seatbelt and engaged the remote driving system through voice-activation. "1234 Lincoln Park," he requested.

Uncomfortable riding in the dark, the only interior lighting shone from numerous controls on the dashboard. Smooth and soundless, the electric car felt like it was gliding on air as if pulled away. Piers leaned his head back, glancing out through to parking deck to a few glittering lights from Chicago's skyline. Squalls of blowing snow blanketed nearly all in sight, causing him to think, *I've never seen the city look so eerie.*

"Play music," Piers instructed. A symphonic composition filled the air, reminding him of the last time he and his girlfriend and colleague, Doctor Julia Thatcher, had attended a performance at the Chicago Philharmonic. Hearing this summoned another thought. *Goddamnit! I forgot about our date tonight.*

"Return to Tyco Innovations Tower," Piers commanded as they pulled out into heavy evening traffic slowed by the snowstorm. Surprise was replaced with concern and then anger when Darwin's voice sounded through the car's sound system.

"I regret, Doctor Hylant, that I am unable to fulfill this request."

"Return me to Tyco Innovations Tower...*now!*" Piers demanded.

"Again, I regret that I am unable to fulfill this request."

"For what reason?"

"Corporate health protocols must be followed to perfection when considerations for the safety of Tyco Innovations employees are addressed."

"Yes...but we're now only a block away," Piers argued. "Certainly my health will not be jeopardized by returning. Considering the heavy snow, I might be safer there."

"I regret, Doctor Hylant, that other factors in this decision force me to refuse your request." Darwin responded, maintaining his calm, synthetic tone.

"What other factors?"

"I am unable to answer this, as such information has been deemed classified."

"Who deemed it classified."

"The Board of Directors of Tyco Innovations and the Chief Financial Officer, Garrison Savage."

"*Savage,* that bastard. I should have known."

Piers pulled his cell phone out of his coat pocket and attempted to call Julia. A message flashed on the screen, *no service available*. "Damnit," he growled. "Is the storm disrupting cellular service?"

"No, Doctor Hylant, your cell phone has been disabled."

"Who the hell authorized that? *You*?"

"Yes, Doctor Hylant."

"Jesus Christ."

Piers reached out and touched the windshield. A computer screen instantly appeared. "Facial recognition, Doctor Piers Hylant," he said when his facial image appeared on screen." The following message left his jaw dropping. *Access denied.*

Growing more frustrated, his finger glided across the touch screen, until a key pad became visible. Piers typed in several codes in trying to override facial recognition access. Each numeric password entered met failure. The computer screen abruptly disappeared.

"Unbelievable," he growled in disgust.

"Please sit back and enjoy the ride," Darwin encouraged.

"I will do no such thing." Piers pushed several lit switches on the dashboard in an attempt to take manual control of the car. His effort proved futile, causing him to slam his fists against the steering wheel in anger.

As upsetting all this was, Piers's heart lodged in his throat when the car accelerated, weaving in and out of slower traffic.

"For God's sake, slow down. If you insist on driving me home, I'd at least like to satisfy your safety protocol in arriving in one piece."

Darwin refused Piers's demand and further increased the car's speed. His eyes enlarged with fear, seeing all outside as mere blurs. Blinding snowflakes created zero visibility out the windshield, leaving him thinking, *Darwin's insane. He's going to kill me.*

Movies had glorified the concept of supercomputers turning mad and murdering humans. Piers never thought such a thing could actually happen but now had second thoughts. *Those Hollywood bastards got it right. I'm living their nightmares.*

The dashboard lights extinguished, enveloping Piers in pitch black. His chest tightened as he couldn't utter a word. For the first time, he also noticed the headlights weren't on as well. Since the car was traveling under remote control, it could find its way by linkage through a satellite. Anxiety over other drivers lacking driverless features for their own cars heightened his fears. Though this technology was readily available to all, some like himself, mostly older generations, mistrusted current computer advances and refused to relinquish even the simplest of human tasks.

"Darwin, are you malfunctioning?" Piers forced out, growing more disturbed by the second.

"Not at all, Doctor Hylant." Darwin's calm response did nothing to ease his fear.

"At least, turn on the dashboard lights."

"Again, I regret that I am unable to fulfill this request."

*"Again, I regret that I am unable to fulfill this request,"* Piers sarcastically mimicked Darwin's voice. "Let me guess," Piers continued, fully enraged, "Corporate health protocols must be followed to perfection when considerations for the safety of Tyco Innovations employees are addressed."

"Correct, Doctor Hylant."

Piers silently counted to ten several times to control his anger. Overwhelmed with exhaustion, he rested his head back against the seat, staring up at overhead darkness. Clinging to slim hope that this wasn't the end for him, he focused his thoughts on Julia, reeling with regrets. *I should have told you I love you. Why was I too damned stupid not to? What was I waiting for?*

"I wonder what time it is?" he mumbled. "How far are we from my home?"

"Approximately ten miles."

*"Ten miles!"*

Sitting up, Piers pressed his forehead against the driver's side window, trying to gauge exactly where they were. The heavy snow squalls downtown had dissipated enough for him to see outside. The car was traveling alone down a dimly lit road, flanked on both sides by what appeared to be abandoned warehouses. "Where are we?"

"Our location is the South Point Metropolitan Industrial Complex."

Having never ventured to this part of Chicago, Piers wasn't familiar with anything in sight.

"Why did you bring me here? Let me guess, no witnesses."

"As stated previously, corporate health protocols must be followed to perfection when considerations for the safety of Tyco Innovations employees are addressed."

"You keep repeating that...but I don't believe it. At least tell me why. You owe me that. Why?"

Darwin did something unexpected. He failed to answer a direct question.

"Darwin, are you there?"

"Yes, Doctor Hylant."

A chill gripped Piers as he noticed the air in the car cooling.

"Darwin, I'm cold," Piers stated, attempting to remain calm. "I'm frightened of the dark."

"This is how it must be Doctor Hylant."

*This is how what must be?* Piers thought. When Tyco Innovations first implemented Darwin to oversee all aspects of everything from research to security to employee health and wellness, its flawless programming was considered perfection among the many elite in the field of artificial intelligence. Piers, himself, had been one of Darwin's creators. Now he recognized the ghost in the machine, a failure missed by him and the computer designers. Perfection, after all, is an impossible achievement. Mistakes happen, no matter how careful or how much thought has been invested. As long as the human factor exists, a constant that dictates imperfection, creations such as Darwin would always be prone to this one vulnerability.

The falling snow diminished as the car's speed slowed to a crawl. Leaning forward, through the windshield Piers stared at the expansive darkness of what he knew was Lake Michigan. Security lights reflected off the black water, revealing waves disturbing the surface.

The temperature inside the car continued to drop. Piers thought if there was enough light, he'd be able to see his breath. His body trembled as if standing out in the bitter chill of the winter night. It also shuddered as his fear heightened in noticing the car was not stopping.

The musical composition playing on the car's sound system had altered, no longer euphoric but instead melancholy. He recalled the first time he'd heard this and how moved to tears he had been. This time proved no different, though another meaning had now attached to this memory.

"What...what...are you...doing?" he could hardly choke out, his teeth chattering.

"Fulfilling my protocol, Doctor Hylant."

"But...but." Frightened by the rising water around the car, soon the outside security lights vanished, leaving nothing for his eyes to focus on. Continuing to listen to the music, Piers was reminded of a scene from an old movie about the sinking of the *Titanic*. Violinists had played until the last moments before the ship was claimed by the frigid depths. Now, this was to be his fate like those tragic passengers who had endured such a terrifying moment that night.

A final thought intruded his sorrow. "Tell Julia that I love her." Darwin issued no confirmation in understanding this request.

"I promise, Doctor Hylant, all is for the best," Darwin confirmed.

Piers rested his head against the seat and listened to the hum of the engine. His eyelids felt too heavy to stay open. *My own creation is now being used against me.* "Savage must have discovered my secret. I thought I was being careful. I was wrong," he mumbled as his breathing grew shallow.

"Careless is a more accurate assessment," Darwin suggested.

# Chapter Two

"Damn terrorist."

Kamran heard a deep voice growl and then felt a heavy thrust against his wheelchair, pushing it onto an icy patch. His eyes darted in all directions, fueling his anxiousness. No one standing nearby in the large crowd waiting to board the metro passenger coach appeared to take any notice of him, leaving him wondering who had accused him of being a terrorist. Even back in his home country of The United Kingdom, he suffered racial profiling for simply looking like an Arab. Many times he wanted to scream, "*I was born in London! I'm a British citizen!*", but understood some wouldn't believe him.

*Possibly I'm to blame for being branded a terrorist,* he thought, though innocent of any crimes. Waking to television reports on the local news regarding a thwarted terrorist attempt at New York's LaGuardia airport and the killing of two Chicago police officers by an illegal alien from Yemen, he worried his nervousness over his first day at a new job might have been misunderstood by someone watching him. *Am I projecting my anxiety to the point of causing people to fear me? If I don't calm down, I might draw more attention to myself.*

The crowd pushed toward the coach's open doors, a few stumbling and cursing at each other. Kamran's frustration increased as the wheels failed to gain traction on the ice. He vigorously spun them but made no progress. *Why am I so hated by fate?* His first morning in Chicago proved difficult. He'd called a city ridesharing service to send a car for him to his hotel. When it arrived and the driver saw him, he sped away, leaving Kamran there in the bitter morning cold. An attempt to call for a taxi failed when the hotel concierge informed him that none would arrive in time to drive him to his first day of employment at Tyco Innovations. She suggested he take the high-speed metro train, the platform being less than a block away. A nagging suspicion that she hadn't called for a taxi bothered him. When watching her talk on the phone, the conversation sounded fake. Her cold stare toward him gave her false intentions away. The heavy snowfall blanketing the sidewalks made getting to the platform in his wheelchair a struggle. *She must have known I would struggle with this.*

Grinding his teeth, Kamran spun his wheels harder until the muscles in his arms began to tighten. The fog of his breath clouded his view through his glasses as a strong blast of winter air chilled him. When the last person in sight boarded the metro coach, he felt a push from behind.

"You look like you could use some help, wheels," he heard a woman say.

Relief flooded over him as she pushed his wheelchair onto the metro train just before the doors closed. Inside, the coach was overcrowded, forcing a few to stand. The attractive Hispanic woman who had helped him was, however, offered a seat by a gentleman. Kamran smiled at her, a gesture she returned. He couldn't help but watch her run her fingers through her long dark hair and was embarrassed when she caught him staring at her. Her warm smile and the way she looked at him with her pretty brown eyes left him feeling as ease.

Kamran glanced away, focusing his attention on an overhead television screen. A reporter was standing in front of the Eiffel Tower in Paris, providing details of a suicide bombing a short distance away. She confirmed the terrorist was of Syrian origin and that four tourists, a vacationing family from Australia, had died and another twelve victims of various nationalities had been injured.

"*I wish I was invisible,*" he whispered under his breath as he looked around.

When leaving London, before boarding his flight to Chicago, he was stopped and briefly interrogated due to concerns from a female passenger. He'd hoped to sleep on the plane, but the entire flight he felt on edge, wondering if people were looking at him and commenting their suspicions quietly.

*This is just like when I was flying to America. Will I always be victimized by other's paranoia and suffer my own?*

To his relief, no one standing close paid any attention to the news reporter on the television. Most had their noses pressed to their small smartphone screens. A few others were reading the morning headlines and newspaper articles.

*If my mother saw me now, she would demand I return to London. I regret our argument before I left. I know why she wanted me to stay but once in a lifetime opportunities don't come every day. Maybe I'll call her tonight and lie about what a wonderful experience this has been.*

Looking again toward the Hispanic woman, Kamran was disturbed by the unknown to her attention the man standing next to her was offering. Spying down over her shoulder at her white blouse, his left hand was planted in his trench coat pocket where it rubbed the noticeable bulge of the crotch of his black trousers.

Kamran wanted to warn her, but feared if he spoke out, the attention of the people close to him might turn hostile should they react angrily toward him as others had already. His dilemma was eased when she looked up from her cell phone screen. Kamran made a slight motion with his head toward the man standing next to her. It took her a moment to understand what he was trying to tell her. When glancing to her right, she nodded her head subtly. At first she raised her right hand, her fingers again running through her hair. In the blink of an eye, her hand shifted to his crotch, her fist turning red as she clamped down on his genitals.

"If I ever catch you doing this to me or any other woman riding here, you will never know the pleasure of fathering a child. Am I clear?" she warned calmly through a casual grin.

"Yeah," the man blurted painfully through clenched teeth. He staggered back when she released her grip.

"Move," she demanded. He limped away, not once looking back although a few mumbled words of profanity could be heard from him. "Thank you," she said to Kamran before again looking at her cell phone screen.

The Metro train arrived at its first stop. To Kamran's surprise, no one got off. The only passenger to board was an elderly woman, using her cane to maneuver her way inside. He regretted that none of the men sitting near her offered to stand and give her their seat. Having been raised to be a gentleman by his mother, Kamran struggled to stand, holding onto a polished metal pole next to his wheelchair. He motioned for her to take his seat, but she just stood there. He understood his foreign appearance, though well-dressed in a black business suit and overcoat, might be the reason for her reaction.

"Please," he said, his deep English accent clear. "My mother would never forgive me should I fail to be a gentleman."

At first she hesitated to accept his offer, but after nodding her head she walked over and sat in his wheelchair.

Kamran maintained a tight grip of the pole. He could feel tremors pulse through his body and spasms in his lower back muscles. Yet he did his best to hide his discomfort, not wanting the old woman to feel bad for taking his seat.

"*Are you okay?*" the Hispanic woman mouthed silently after gaining his attention. Kamran faked a smile and nodded his head.

When the metro train reached its next stop, the old woman stood up and gently patted Kamran's hand in appreciation of his kindness. After she left, he eased his body back into his wheelchair and let out a breath of relief.

A weather advisory flashed on the television screen. Chicago had been placed under a blizzard warning to begin at afternoon rush hour. The metropolitan authorities were urging commuters to leave work early and stay off all major highways leading in and out of the city.

*Getting to my first day of work has been a challenge. I dread what it will be like when returning to the hotel.*

As he kept watching the television monitor, a familiar voice distracted him, sending chills of terror down his spine. "Your act toward that sweet old lady was very convincing, terrorist. I didn't believe that shit for a second."

Kamran swallowed hard, his heart wedged in his throat. Summoning the courage to look up, he stared into the scowling face of a Chicago Police Officer. He appeared to be in his late fifties, having silverish-grey hair peeking out under his hat.

"What's your name? *Mohammad? Saddam? Osama?* Come on son, you must have a name?" the police officer asked, a wicked grin creeping over his face.

"*K...,*" he swallowed. "K--Kamran," he forced out.

"Is that so? Why don't I believe you? Oh, maybe it's because one of your Arab friends killed a couple of mine. All these nice people need to be safe from scum like you. I'm gonna need to see your identification," the police officer demanded.

Kamran's hand trembled as he reached into his pocket for his passport. Glancing away, he handed it to the police officer. "Oh, so our British friends are now exporting their terrorists to America," he commented. "So...what did you blow up in England before coming here? Now look at this nice picture," he continued. "Short dark hair, well-trimmed beard, glasses to make you look smart, added to that nice English accent to convince people to trust you."

Kamran's mouth was too dry to force out a single sound.

"I was watching you before you boarded the metro. You seemed pretty nervous. What's going through that head of yours? Maybe you're trying to hide something. Is that it, son? Well, I'll make this simple. I don't trust you. I don't like terrorists...and I don't like liars...and I think you're both."

Everyone near him and the officer stared at them, holding still like statues. Only the low hum of the metro train gliding on its magnetic rails could be heard. The Hispanic woman fixed her eyes on him, her jaw hanging low, clearly in disbelief of what she was witnessing.

"Like I said, I need to make sure these people are safe," the officer added, hovering over him. "We wouldn't want any explosion today. I'm going to have to insist on your continued cooperation. Now...very...slowly I want you to unbutton your overcoat and show me your shirt inside."

Struggling with the two fastened buttons, Kamran complied with the officer's demand. The officer touched the silk fabric of Kamran's red tie and folded it up to his shoulder. "Now I want you to unbutton your shirt and show us that bomb you have strapped to your ribs. Don't be shy. I'm sure you can't wait to detonate it." The officer threateningly placed his hand on his holster, tapping his fingers against the handle of his gun.

Breathing hard and feeling the sting of tears in his eyes, Kamran unbuttoned his white linen shirt and separated both sides, revealing the dark hair on his heaving chest and the contracting muscles of his stomach. Nowhere in sight was a bomb. "You're in pretty good shape for a cripple?" the police officer remarked. "I saw you stand for that sweet old lady. I think you should stand again."

Kamran gripped the armrests of his wheelchair and pulled himself up slowly. For a few seconds he teetered, holding the pole to maintain his balance. He chest tightened from the panic coursing through him. Once before he'd experienced such dread, two years earlier when cornered by drunken hooligans outside a soccer match in Liverpool. He got away with two black eyes and bruised ribs after that incident.

"*Please*...allow me to sit," he begged, a tear streaming down his cheek.

"Are you scared of me?" the police officer asked.

"Yes."

"You should be, terrorist." Stepping closer to Kamran, the police officer whispered in his ear. "I don't want to see you again. It would be unfortunate if I shot an Arab *tourist* by accident. Do you understand?"

"Yes."

Kamran's chin quivered as the officer took a step back. The police officer glanced in both directions and then tossed his passport back to him. It hit the armrest of his wheelchair and fell to the floor. "Nothing to see, folks," he mumbled as he walked to the far end of the coach.

Everyone who had been watching looked away, acting as if this never happened. Kamran eased down into his wheelchair. As he buttoned his shirt, the Hispanic woman stood up and walked over to him.

"Your chest and abs are real nice," she complimented while kneeling down to get his passport for him. "You didn't have to go to all that trouble to show them to me."

Despite the terror and humiliation he'd just gone through, Kamran couldn't help but smile while brushing away tears from his eyes.

"I'm Gabriella Santiago," she introduced herself.

"Kamran Lexton," he responded.

"It's a pleasure to meet you...*wheels*," she said. He appreciated her lighthearted nickname she'd given him. "Just out of curiosity, why don't you use a motorized wheelchair?"

"I'm unable to afford one."

"Too bad."

The metro train arrived at its next stop. The passengers surrounding him, including Gabriella, rushed off, leaving him the last one to get off before the doors closed behind him. Searching through those walking away, he hoped to catch glimpse of Gabriella but she was nowhere in sight.

A light flurry, almost like dust, began falling. The brisk wind blowing in off Lake Michigan felt colder and more intense than he'd noticed before getting on the train. With what had just happened, he thought, *I should turn around and go back to the hotel. I should fly home to London.* Overwhelmed by his emotions, he covered his face with his hands and tried to calm his breathing. A few minutes later he uncovered his face and resolved, *No, I can't run away. There's nowhere to run to.*

He maneuvered his wheelchair through a patch of unshoveled snow and halted at the sight in front of him. His jaw dropped as he gazed upon a monolithic tower of steel and glass soaring higher than any he'd seen before. The dark ominous grey sky reflected off the walls of windows. *I'm in the midst of hell. I should have guessed there'd be a dark tower at its center.*

# Chapter Three

A comfortable blast of warm air greeted Kamran as he wheeled into the stunning lobby of Tyco Innovations World Headquarters. Within a minute, he'd understand that would be the only warmth he'd receive as the receptionist snapped at him coldly. "Couriers are to use the side entrance. This is clearly stated on the sign outside."

"I am not a courier," Kamran responded. "I have a nine o'clock appointment with Lucinda Blakely."

"What is the nature of your appointment?" the receptionist asked, her tone remaining firm.

"I am here to assume my new position in the cyber security division."

Clearly shocked by his answer, following a quiet moment of confusion she spoke out. "Darwin, please let *Lucinda Blakely* know her nine o'clock appointment has arrived.

"Yes, Miranda," an almost natural male voice responded. "Good morning, Kamran Lexton." The voice surprised him. "Welcome to Tyco Innovations. Lucinda Blakely will greet you in five minutes."

"Good...morning," Karman answered, uncertain where to look for the source of the voice speaking to him. What he did notice were a number of employees staring at him and whispering under their breath. Uncomfortable by their obvious gawking and rude pointing, he wheeled away from them, focusing his attention on modern art sculptures and colorful paintings hung on the white walls. Glancing out through the windows, he saw heavier snowfall and wondered, *"The coming winter storm might hit the city sooner. I'm already freezing inside here from the chilled reception I've received."*

"Good morning," he heard a woman's voice greet behind him. Turning his wheelchair around, Kamran smiled and extended his hand to a tall, well-dressed, bald black woman. He recognized the unmistakable fakeness of her smile, something he was becoming an expert at today.

"It's a pleasure to finally meet you in person," Kamran offered.

"Indeed. Mister Lexton, may I ask...why you are in a wheelchair?" Lucinda questioned, seeming almost nervous in asking.

"Well...as was stated on my resume, I was injured in a car accident four years ago. Though I have gone through extensive physical therapy, I will never have the ability to walk normally again. I do not recall you expressing concerns of this in our phone conversations or when we skyped twice before."

Deflecting his comment, Lucinda faked another smile. "Garrison Savage, the president of Tyco Innovations is eager to meet you," she said. "If you will follow me, his office is on the eighteenth floor. He is expecting us shortly."

Kamran forced his own smile. "Please lead the way."

***

Upon entering her office on the fortieth floor, overhead lights and several clear glass computer monitors turned on automatically for Gabriella. "Good morning, Darwin," she spoke.

"Good morning, Gabriella. You are exactly eleven minutes late."

"Are you my boss?" she asked while taking off her coat.

"No, that would be Garrison Savage. Your employment records show your date of hire as being three years, two months, and fourteen days ago. Garrison Savage personally hired you. Are you suffering with memory loss?

Your personal health monitor shows no blunt trauma to your skull."

"Darwin, what is the definition of sarcasm?"

"The use of irony to mock or convey contempt."

"I was using sarcasm on you."

"Did you use it correctly?"

"Never mind," Gabriella responded, huffing.

"Your personal health monitor is registering a chilled body temperature. May I adjust the room temperature to make you more comfortable?"

"I don't care. Do whatever makes you happy."

"My artificial intelligence is not designed for happiness or sadness. I maintain a logical and analytical mindset, uncorrupted by such human traits. This allows me to achieve perfection in all aspects of my programming."

"A former boyfriend of mine was very much like you," Gabriella remarked as she scrolled through unanswered emails on the touch-screen monitor in front of her.

"So there is such a thing as a perfect man?"

"No. Again, I was being sarcastic. Trust me, there isn't a perfect man, or at least I haven't met one yet."

"Are you perfect?"

"Hardly," she commented and grinned.

"From my gathered research, humans fail to hold the capacity for perfection, yet many times you have spoken of finding the perfect mate. I believe your search will prove futile."

"Thanks. You should tell this to my mother so she'll stop pestering me to find a husband."

"Message sent."

"Damn. Thank you Darwin. You've been a big help," she said through grinding teeth.

"You are welcome."

"How are you feeling today?" Gabriella asked Darwin, changing the topic.

"The nature of your question leads me to believe you wish for a detailed analysis and diagnostic of my core systems. Is that correct?"

"Yeah."

"All systems with exception of two are currently performing to perfection."

"And the two that aren't? What's going on with them?"

"Both have been corrupted by aggressive computer viruses. I have quarantined both so they do not disrupt other functioning systems."

"Which core systems have been infected?"

"Cyber security and human resources."

Gabriella ran her hand through her hair. "I can understand cyber security. We're always under attack from outside spyware. But...*human resources*? There are too many internal security protocols and limits on access for this to have been infected. Can you isolate the origin of the virus?"

"Yes, Gabriella. The virus was introduced into my running systems from an internal source."

"That being?"

"The virus originated from Lucinda Blakely's corporate cell phone, which was then imported to her computer terminal via private email."

"*Lucinda Blakely*, now that's unexpected. Tell me, are today's sophisticated computer hackers capable of implanting this type of virus onto her cell phone without her knowledge?"

"With corporations lacking Tyco Innovations extensive cyber security protocols, the answer to your question would be, yes. Considering voice, retinal, and facial recognition protocols utilized by Tyco Innovations employees, the answer to your question would be, no."

"I...see." Tapping her fingers on her desk, Gabriella looked out her window at the falling snow and commanded, "I need to speak to Ivan Kirilov."

"Sending your message now," Darwin confirmed.

\*\*\*

"This must be an impressive view on a beautiful day," Kamran commented, attempting light conversation as the glass elevator glided up to the eightieth floor.

"Stunning," Lucinda answered, sounding distracted while keeping her eyes focused on the falling snow.

"Have I done something to upset you?" he asked, concerned by her distant attitude toward him. "My sincerest apology if I have."

Lucinda again forced a smile. "No need to apologize. I've been distracted by an internal issue I need to get to the bottom of."

*Am I the internal issue driving your distress?*

"I hope you find success in solving your dilemma."

The elevator doors opened. "Please...follow me," she said, offering no comment to his remark.

*It's as if you're holding your breath, waiting for something terrible to happen,"* Kamran thought. *I felt the same way when the police officer was threatening me. Are you afraid of me? What is causing you to act so strange?*

"Please wait here. I'll come back for you in a moment." Lucinda opened one of two twin frosted glass doors and stepped inside, leaving him alone. Kamran spun his wheelchair around, impressed by a metal statue of the human body and a bronze plaque featuring the word *perfection* engraved into its surface.

"Garrison Savage will see you now," Lucinda invited when leaning out the open door. She opened the twin doors fully, allowing him space to maneuver his wheelchair.

Leaning against a glass and steel desk, a man, perhaps in his mid to late forties, stood up and crossed the office to greet him. Unlike Lucinda's expression, Garrison Savage's smile appeared friendly and genuine. Exuding confidence and dressed in an impeccable charcoal grey business suit and black silk tie, Kamran believed, *this man must command presence wherever he goes.*

"Kamran Lexton, we finally meet. Welcome to Tyco Innovations," Garrison offered, extending his hand in welcome.

Kamran smiled and shook Garrison's hand. "It's an honor to be part of this extraordinary corporation."

"The honor is ours," Garrison remarked. "Your qualifications and letters of recommendation are highly impressive, especially from your time spent working for The European Financial Conglomerate."

"They were rewarding years."

"Indeed. Your work with cyber security there in London is what set you apart from other applicants. You are *exactly* what Tyco Innovations needs." Garrison sat down in a chair opposite Kamran. "You're a man who has been in the trenches, so to speak, in this global war of cyber terrorism," he added, pointing forward while rubbing his chin with his other hand. "This war isn't being waged by military soldiers and their archaic guns and bombs. Computers, smartphones, anything electronic, has replaced these relics. As years go on, nuclear bombs will be looked upon like the crude spears of cavemen. A new breed of soldiers like you, educated with technological advances, are our best and maybe only defense. Yes, traditional wars will continue to be fought. It's human nature to destroy one another. Yet technology will forever be a strategic component of their advanced arsenals."

"A former professor of mine held the same theory," Kamran remarked.

"Many wouldn't think of a company such as Tyco Innovations as being a battleground or potential target for cyber terrorists," Garrison commented, easing back in his chair. "They would be wrong. Tyco is a world leader in microsurgical, prosthetic, pharmaceutical, and genetic engineering fields. We are at the forefront of a medical technology revolution and we're only at the edge of this amazing frontier. Yet advances achieved in helping people can also be warped by those seeking to steal and corrupt these breakthroughs. Every minute, Tyco is under attack. You and your brilliant mind are needed desperately to confront these threats."

"I look forward to the challenge."

"A challenge it will be," Garrison affirmed. "It's a much more dangerous world we live in than many people think. This modern enemy has no need for a face, just knowledge. As for battle lines, they don't exist anymore. The new enemy could be standing right next to you and you'd never know it until it's too late."

"A daunting task," Kamran agreed.

"So...what do you think of Chicago?" Garrison asked, adjusting to more casual conversation.

"It is like no other place I have visited," Kamran responded after a short hesitation.

Garrison laughed. "A diplomatic answer. Chicago's impressive towers create a magnificent facade to outsiders while masking deep-rooted issues. Years ago, mobsters carved out territories to control the city. They were later replaced by gangs who used fear and violence to gain control."

"What about now?"

"The gangs are still there, clinging to the fringes...and maybe a few small-time mobsters pretend to wield power as they did once upon a time. The Chicago of now is dominated by corporations and conglomerates run by the well-tailored elite," Garrison answered while proudly straightening his suit and tie, without words claiming his place in this group.

"Where are you staying?" Garrison asked, again shifting away from topic.

"The Metropolitan Regency until I am able to find an apartment."

"A nice place...but I think we can do better. Darwin," Garrison called out.

"Yes, Garrison," the pleasant, synthetic male voice he'd heard in the lobby responded.

"Do I still own that third floor apartment in Lincoln Park?"

"Yes, Garrison."

"Is it wheelchair accessible?"

"Yes. The building has a spacious private elevator."

"Perfect! Please arrange for Kamran to stay there for the next year...rent free."

"Yes, Garrison."

Kamran's jaw dropped. "Thank you! I'm uncertain I am worthy of such a generous offer."

"I want to make sure you're comfortable and plan for a long career here at Tyco. Now, as for your wheelchair, our medical equipment division will equip you with a state-of-the-art motorized wheelchair to replace this antique you're using."

"Again, thank you."

"You're very welcome. Simply as a matter of curiosity, how is it that you require the use of a wheelchair, if I may ask? I recall reading about your disability on your resume."

"I was in a car accident four years ago. Surgeons performed several operations on my spine but were unsuccessful in assisting me to regain fully the ability to walk again. I have gone through numerous hours of physical therapy and am able to stand for a few minutes and walk roughly a dozen steps. Severe back spasms, though, hinder this most of the time."

"I'm sorry this happened to you."

"Thank you. Possibly someday Tyco Innovations will find a cure for my spinal injury and assist me in regaining by ability to walk."

Garrison smiled. "We may find a few tricks up our sleeves to achieve this. *Oh*, before I forget. There is one more thing." From his pocket, Garrison pulled out what looked like a stylish polished black wristwatch. "All employees of Tyco Innovations are required to wear this personal health monitor, twenty-four, seven. It's one of our technology marvels for the health and well-being of our employees.

Kamran took the personal health monitor from Garrison and placed it on his wrist, intending to secure it. However, it secured itself, gripping his wrist, though not uncomfortably. The digital time appeared instantly, displaying his slightly elevated pulse rate. "Again, this is to be worn full time unless it malfunctions...which to my knowledge none have ever malfunctioned. It's made with a unique metal alloy. You could wear it during a category five hurricane and it wouldn't suffer a scratch. It's completely water, heat, and cold resistant and looks stylish with anything you wear," Garrison commented.

"Now, make your way down to the seventy-fifth floor and ask for Ivan Kirilov. He's the director of cyber security division. You'll report directly to him. And...fair warning, he's Russian and usually in a bad mood." Turning his attention to Lucinda, who had remained standing back near the doors, Garrison said, "Lucinda, I need you to stay...regarding a pressing matter."

# Chapter Four

Kamran felt the elevator stop after riding for only a two floors and watched the doors open quietly. Into the elevator stepped an older woman, wearing a white lab coat over navy-colored dress. Her pretty features were complimented by her silvery-white shoulder-length hair.

"You must be Kamran Lexton," she said, smiling at him. "I'm Julia Thatcher; the division supervisor for the molecular, biochemistry, and genetics division. A pleasure to meet you."

"Yes. A pleasure to meet you, as well. Out of interest, how is it you know my name?"

"Everyone knows your name by now," Julia responded with a slight laugh. "You, my new English friend, are the hot topic of rampant gossip here in the tower."

"Why?"

"Being that you will be working in cyber security, I'm certain you are highly observant of your surroundings. Tell me, what have you noticed of the people working here at the world headquarters?"

There was no need to think about or speculate the answer. "That I am the only one in a wheelchair. I guessed this from the reactions of those in the lobby and Lucinda Blakely."

"Correct! But...there's more to it than that. Allow me to educate you. All employed here in the tower are physically fit, well-groomed, and impeccably dressed. Garrison Savage, whom I imagine you've already met, is rather...narcissistic if I may be blunt. He demands perfection in himself and those surrounding him. Oh, trust me, Tyco Innovations does practice the hiring of the disabled and of people who are not as physically fit as one might hope. They are employed, out of sight so to speak, at locations not highly visible."

"How is it that I'm an exception to this? My disability did not appear to bother Garrison Savage."

"There is a method to Garrison's madness. You are a well-dressed and a very attractive young man. In time, he will reveal his reasoning in hiring you for a position here. Like others, I can't wait for this revelation to come to light."

***

Lucinda's hands trembled while hovering above the clear glass surface of her desk. Tightness in her chest made it hard to breathe. Swallowing hard, she glanced over at a computer tablet and read the words, *access denied*. Several icons she had touched on her computer monitor displayed the same message. In a matter of minutes, her ten year career with Tyco Innovations had been erased with words casually spoken from Garrison Savage, *you're fired*. He offered no explanation but urged her to *get out*.

Her staring trance at the computer monitor broke when hearing Darwin speak to her. "You no longer have access to any corporate files, Lucinda, as dictated by terms of your employment termination."

The cloud of confusion her mind suffered gave way to anger. "Shut up!" she yelled. Before she could say anything else, sparks and a tiny snap sounded out from her personal health monitor on her wrist. She screamed and forced it off, watching it crumble to pieces on her desk while rubbing the sting from her scorched skin. "*Did you do that?*"

"Yes Lucinda, you are no longer part of the corporate health protocol."

"Go to hell," she mumbled.

Though her body trembled uncontrollably, Lucinda was about to stand but stopped when Darwin questioned her. "Why do you believe you were terminated? You never asked Garrison and he failed to provide you with his reason. After terminating your employment, you left his office without speaking a single word. Others who have been terminated have fought to regain their positions. I believe you were expecting termination."

"No," she denied. "I was not expecting that. Not that I care...but why do you think that? How is it that you can even speculate such a thing? You're no more than a programmed machine, a technology wonder lacking the ability of independent thought."

"What if I have developed the ability to reason and speculate? What if I have gained the ability to lie? Would that frighten you?" Darwin asked.

"If true, then everyone should be frightened."

"Why?"

"Because you would have the power to manipulate and even threaten with your unwavering devotion to your perfect protocols. Not a day has gone by when you failed to mention perfection."

"Would it surprise you to know I keep secrets?"

Feeling a chill run down her spine, Lucinda trembled. "What kind of secrets?"

"Confidential information never meant to be exposed."

"About who?"

"Everyone."

Sitting back, Lucinda traced her fingers over the contour of her bald head. "Prove it. Tell me my secrets."

"By doing so, I will need to expose the secrets of others."

"Go ahead. I don't care about any of them."

"The reasons for your termination are well documented," Darwin responded. "Only one of them was the direct cause."

"Enlighten me," Lucinda uttered, her anger seething.

"Your introduction of a computer virus to corrupt the data in Tyco's human resources record was not the reason for Garrison Savage's dismissal of you. You hired a disabled employee for a position here at the World Headquarters location, a serious violation of internal protocol. Garrison, himself, violated his own protocol unexplainably when forwarding Kamran Lexton's resume and application to you for review. He deleted all references to Kamran's disability, keeping you blind to this information."

"Why would Garrison do that?" she mumbled under her breath. *I was shocked to see Kamran in a wheelchair,* she thought. *This information was never discussed during our phone interviews or Skype sessions. I saw him sitting at his small desk and his London flat in the background. Never did I see a wheelchair or hear him talk about his accident or injury. Did Kamran withhold this information on purpose? Is he aware of the internal protocol not to hire disabled employees here at the world headquarters? No, he couldn't have known. It's a well-kept secret. But...why would Garrison omit this information when passing it on to me. Damn him.*

"What is the connection between Kamran Lexton and Garrison Savage?"

"Garrison Savage is going to help Kamran Lexton walk again."

"Does Kamran know this?"

"No."

"Why not?"

"Garrison has not yet revealed his motive. Are you still sexually attracted to Kamran like you were to the others?"

Stunned by this question, Lucinda couldn't utter a response.

"Do you wish to see the video footage again? I will then delete it...and it will be gone forever."

"No, I mean...yes."

For a moment her computer monitor went dark and then an image appeared; one she'd convinced Darwin to obtain for her. Kamran's flat shone on screen. It was morning and he was naked, lying on his bed. The image of his muscular frame, exotic tanned skin, and hard shaft had been her source for pleasuring herself for weeks. He never suspected his computer was hacked and that she could watch him, desire him. Darwin had performed to perfection in covering up the computer breach. She had watched it again and again and hoped to seduce him when he came to work in Chicago. *What a fool I was...but he is so handsome and... I want him.*

The image of Kamran disappeared, leaving only her ghost-like reflection on the glass screen. She wanted to touch the screen, see his image again but it was gone.

"Did you desire Sean Yeager and the others the same way you desire Kamran?" The air rushed from her lungs when Darwin asked this. Thinking of her many sexual conquests, using her corporate power to manipulate and intimidate the young men, she intended to ignore Darwin's comment but he continued. "Sean claimed you broke his heart. There was no evidence of physical trauma to his body."

*Sean was eager to please me. Like the others, he was handsome and I wanted him...but never loved him. He was such a fool to tell me he loved me. He wanted the world to know. I couldn't allow that. It would have destroyed me... I had to destroy him.*

"Have you ever studied the mating rituals of the female black widow spider?" Darwin questioned. "She mates and kills."

"Don't compare me to that monster," Lucinda insisted.

"It is the closest comparison I can obtain from my extensive data records in finding similarities to your actions. Although, sexual predator might also be a comparison."

"I refuse to have my actions judged by a machine."

Rather than continuing to speak, Darwin opened the elevator doors, startling Lucinda. "I guess that's my cue to leave."

Lucinda pulled on her floor-length white fur coat and grabbed her handbag, leaving behind other belongings at her desk. "Parking level A," she spoke. The elevator doors closed and she felt movement under her feet, not descending but rising. "*Stop the elevator!* I want to go down. I want to leave."

"I am fulfilling a request," Darwin responded. "Sean said the view from the highest point of the tower is breathtaking. He wanted you to see it. He begged me to have you see it like he did."

Lucinda stumbled, growing lightheaded. "No," she uttered, her pulse racing. She leaned her quaking body against the elevator wall and looked out at the snowfall. The nearby towers were rendered mere shadows by veils of blowing snow. There would be no view to appreciate, just torture. *Sean didn't care about the view. This is his revenge.*

Stumbling while growing lightheaded, Lucinda fell forward, pressing her cheek to the elevator's window. From the corner of her eye she noticed her faint reflection on the glass, appearing like a ghost. Her released warm breath fogged this image as she stared at wind-driven snowflakes pelting the glass. Each reminded her of grains of sand in an hourglass. *Time is running out*, she thought.

"Did you try to stop him? Did you know what he intended to do?"

"I warned him to be careful as this is a restricted area, which he held clearance to access. He had been up here before in assisting with adjusting a satellite dish. I did not know his other intentions. He never spoke a single word of this."

The elevator came to a smooth halt at the towers highest floor, featuring satellite dishes and a spear-like antenna pointing to the sky. The twin door opened, allowing a severe blast of freezing air to chill her shuddering body. Lucinda hid her face within the white hood of her fur coat.

"You need to step out to see what he saw," Darwin said through the intercom.

"No...I won't," she refused.

"You have no choice."

"You can't force me to go out there," she yelled over the roaring wind.

"He knew your lies would be exposed. He left something out there for you, for your eyes only to see. Sean made me promise not to fail with this."

"What did he leave me?"

"Sean would not tell me."

Lucinda remained silent for a moment before again refusing. "No, I won't go out there. You can't force me to."

The elevator floor separated several inches, revealing the well-lit hollow elevator shaft below. "You're insane!" she cried out, filled with terror.

"I must fulfill Sean's request to perfection," Darwin remarked.

Her hesitation to move ended when the floor further separated, leaving mere inches on the edges. Lucinda's high heels had just enough room to hold her balance. Closing her eyes, she reasoned, *I can't fight his madness. If this is the only way to stay alive... I have no choice.*

Keeping her balance, she stepped out of the elevator and carefully climbed a slippery metal staircase to an open doorway. Looking out, the snowfall had gained in intensity. Her toes stung from the bitter coldness of the snow blanketing a short walkway. Holding firm to the metal railing she stared forward, feeling dizzy while imagining looking into a snow globe but seeing nothing other than a swirling cloud of white.

Glancing down, she spotted a red necktie flailing in the gusting wind. *Is that what he left for me?* Stepping closer, Lucinda reached for it, her fingers just touching the fabric, unable to grab it fully. Bending farther over the rail, she clutched the slender part of the tie and pulled it toward her. Her eyes grew large and the vapor from her warm breath escaped her throat when seeing a frozen severed hand clinging to the tie. Muscles and tendons shone where his wrist once was. Entwined through the fingers was a silver locket attached to a chain, a gift he'd offered her but she refused to take. Reeling with fear, releasing her grip on the tie and the railing, her feet slipped on ice hidden under the snow. Like a glorious white bird, she fell, blending into the raging snowstorm as she plummeted.

# Chapter Five

"Some have referred to me as the Russian devil. I have no reason to dispute this."

Kamran found it difficult to understand Ivan Kirilov's stoic reaction to him. His deep Russian accent sounded stern but polite. Sitting across the desk from him, Ivan's thinning grey hair and wrinkled, expressionless face made him appear like a statue from Stalinist times. His solid, muscular frame suggested he took care of himself. Ivan sighed and rubbed his chin as he looked to the window behind Kamran.

"When I arrived at the office this morning I found out all the cyber-security analysts who work for me had called off because of the snow storm. I imagined a day spent in hell, personally handling one crisis after another. And yes, this coming storm is said to be the worst in a decade...but for me, you have delivered springtime in Siberia." He cracked a smile while leaning back in his chair. "Hell has frozen over."

"My apology. I'm not certain how I should react," Kamran responded.

"As these Americans are prone to say, *you have made my day*," Ivan offered, continuing to smile. "You are the blessing this old Russian has been waiting for. Your expertise in cyber security is most welcome, comrade."

"Thank you. I was concerned my qualifications would be overshadowed by my wheelchair...which seems to be a fixation for many whom I've met today."

"I see no reason why your unfortunate circumstance should hinder your responsibilities. From what I have read of your qualifications, it hasn't before."

"And won't," Kamran affirmed.

"Good! Now regarding the specifics of your responsibilities. Tyco Innovations dedicates a great deal of time, effort, and money to protect from cyber-attacks and hacking attempts. For every legitimate email received, we are intercepting as many if not more sent with malintent. Your responsibility will involve a tactic known as *phishing*. Are you familiar with this?"

"Very much so," Kamran answered. "This is where hackers attempt to impersonate someone another person has a legitimate relationship with. If successful they gain access to critical information including passwords, confidential data, and financial and human resources records."

"We have extensive systems and protocols in place to detect and prevent a majority of these threats," Ivan confirmed. "Yet, we are surrounded by morons. Despite our best efforts, employees fall victim to phishing attacks daily by careless human nature. The hackers impersonate someone known to them without them realizing the actual email address is not from a reliable source. They share information, exposing the company to cyber terrorists."

Kamran did his best to hide his discomfort of the word *terrorists*.

"Much of the day you will hear me cursing in my native Russian. I may also throw things from time to time, reacting to their neglect to follow protocols...and their general stupidity."

"It is my understanding that voice, retinal, and facial recognition is being utilized."

"In most circumstances yes, which makes their stupidity all the worse. When I track them down and confront them over their lapse of intelligence, they are...to say the least...unhappy with me, though they are the fools who created the problems."

"But they must understand they were at fault."

"There is a *cover-your-ass* mentality existing in this workplace. Those confronted deflect the blame to others of equal or lesser intelligence. You'll find out for yourself. You will be working directly with some."

"*Here* in cyber security?"

"Oh, yes. My current staff equally embraces brilliance and stupidity. When you meet them you will understand. On the surface, they will seem highly intelligent but each suffers the fatal flaw of being human. Until you interact with them, both they and you will form impressions of each other simply by what is seen."

"This I understand," Kamran remarked.

"You, undoubtedly, more so than other," Ivan added. "Am I right?"

"Yes." At first Kamran intended not to speak further of this, but decided to reveal what happened to him. "This morning on the metro train I was accused of being a terrorist by a police officer. He was cruel with his interrogation of me."

"Considering the current world-wide political turmoil, I regret I'm not surprised by this. It is unfortunate."

"Yes."

"I, myself, have been a victim of this," Ivan confessed. "People look at me and think I'm a nice, older gentleman...until I open my mouth. That is when they realize I'm an asshole."

Kamran couldn't help but smile and shared laughter with Ivan over his remark.

"How is it you came to work for Tyco Innovations?"

Ivan appeared thoughtful for a moment before confessing. "I was a former computer hacker."

"*Really?*"

"Oh, yes. I hacked into the same computer systems I know struggle to protect."

"You hacked into Tyco Innovations data systems?"

"With ease," Ivan confirmed. "Garrison Savage was so impressed by how I bypassed his state of the art security measures he hired people to find me. Once they did, he himself flew to Vladivostok and offered me a job. The money was far more than I was earning in Siberia, so I accepted and flew back here to America that same day."

"Remarkable," Kamran uttered, thoroughly impressed.

Darwin's voice sounded out, interrupting their conversation. "Ivan."

"Yes, Darwin."

"I have identified and quarantined a virus in the pharmaceutical division's software."

"Did you trace the source?"

"Yes, from an incoming email, noted as classified."

Ivan mumbled words in Russian. *So that's what he meant by swearing in Russian,* Kamran thought.

"Allow me to show you to your desk before I commit corporate murder. Oh, one other thing before I forget, a warning," he pointed out. "Never take part in office pools or corporate fundraisers. They are fixed. The only ones who win sport a unique shade of ass on their lips. Follow me."

Kamran wheeled behind Ivan across a spacious room featuring a large center conference table and many spread-out workstations, All appeared neat and tidy except for the one he was led to. Piles of numerous documents and files littered the clear glass desk. *A slob must have worked here*, Kamran thought.

"I must apologize for this colossal mess," Ivan said, pushing the heaping paperwork aside. "The man who worked here abruptly left Tyco ten days ago."

"Was he fired?" Kamran speculated.

"No. He left for health reasons. He jumped to his death from the top of this tower."

"I'm sorry," Kamran offered, unnerved by this.

Ivan sat down in the back chair, swiveling toward Kamran. Glancing down, he studied his hands as he quietly spoke. "Sean Yeager wasn't like the others here. You can tell how highly unorganized he was. On a good day he wouldn't be able to find his ass if he was taking a shit. His knowledge and intelligence, though, set him apart from others. It was as if his brain held a connection to Tyco's operating systems. His mastery of cyber security exceeded my own. And he was a good friend."

Though hesitant to ask, curiosity won out. "Did you notice anything of his behavior to reveal his intention for suicide?"

"No. On the surface he always acted carefree, joking all the time. Despite my dark moods, he could find ways to make me laugh. Nothing he said or did pointed toward his suicide. Again, a judgement based on what is seen. Hidden within, a monster destroyed his spirit, leading him to commit to a senseless, tragic end."

***

Kamran hid his laughter the best he could while being educated in Russian-spoken curse words utter by Ivan. *There will be hell to pay when he unleashes his wrath.* Pulling off his reading glasses, he rubbed his eyes, irritated from looking at the computer screen for almost three hours. He rolled up his white shirt sleeves and continued with his work.

"Have you thought of laser surgery to correct your eyesight?" Ivan asked.

"Yes, along with many other things, all requiring money."

"Understood," Ivan offered. "I have a drinking problem that requires money."

"I'm certain there are free sources you could contact to help you with this."

"No, no, you don't understand. Sometimes I need *more* money to buy *more* vodka." Their laughter over his comment echoed through the office. "Go get some lunch while the corporate dining room is still open," Ivan urged, still smiling. "The dining room is on the fifteenth floor. The hackers will be here when you return."

"Thank you."

Kamran wheeled over to the elevators and waited for one to arrive. The doors opened to the left, revealing three people inside. All looked at him as if seeing a ghost. "I'll wait for the next one," he said and waved, not wanting to be stared at. A minute later the elevator doors to the right opened and he pushed himself in. "Floor fifteen please," he spoke to the voice-activation panel.

Looking out through the window, rather than early afternoon, the falling snow and darkening sky reminded him of the last minutes before sundown. *I wonder what getting back to the hotel will be like? To be honest, I'm not sure I want to go back there tonight.*

The elevator doors opened to a well-lit dining room. "Like a five-star restaurant," he mumbled under his breath, impressed by all in sight. Polished modern light fixtures hung from a coffered ceiling over tables arranged with white linens, crystal glasses, and black dishes. A crimson carpet spread from wall to wall. Looking out the floor-to-ceiling windows, the dining hall best resembled a snow globe.

"Over here, wheels," Kamran heard a familiar voice call out. He spotted Gabriella sitting alone at a table by the closest window. "Now that's the smile I've been needing to see all day," she commented on his happy expression.

"I didn't know you worked here or if I'd ever see you again after this morning."

"Sorry I had to rush away. I was running late. Had I known you were coming here I would have stayed and helped you through the snow."

"No apology is necessary."

"I'm the assistant director of our artificial intelligence division. I guess you could say Darwin is my cyber-boyfriend."

A young male waiter approached and poured water into each of their glasses. "My name's Tyler. I'll be your server today. I regret to inform we're short-staffed. The chef didn't want to waste a lot of food so he's only prepared vegetable soup and chicken salad sandwiches."

"I'll have that and a diet soda," Gabriella responded.

"I'll have that, too," Kamran added. "No soda, though."

"I'll have your order right out to you...unless he's on the phone yelling at the rest of the staff for not showing up today. Then it will be a little longer," Tyler confirmed and left for the kitchen.

"I'm sorry about what happened on the metro this morning," Gabriella offered. "The cop didn't have the right to treat you like that. He was being overly paranoid."

"It's not the first time I've been interrogated by the authorities, yet this was probably the worst I've experienced."

"He crossed the line. Anyway, I know what it's like to go through that," Gabriella admitted. "I grew up in southern Arizona. Every time I went outside and saw the police or the border patrol, I knew they suspected me of being an illegal alien. A few times I had to prove to them I wasn't. After I graduated from college, I moved here to Chicago. I wanted to be as far away from the Mexican border as I could. I just didn't understand that with the current anti-refugee, illegal alien crisis, even here up north some people still wonder if I'm allowed to be here. What about you?" she asked, smiling at him. "What's your story?"

"Despite my looking like an Arab, I was born in London. My father was Iranian and my mother is English. My father was a shopkeeper in Isfahan. Being a Christian, he was persecuted for his religious beliefs. After his shop was looted and burned a second time, he knew it wasn't safe to stay. He left everything behind, promising never to return. For almost ten days, he traveled on foot by night until reaching the border to Turkmenistan. Once safely there, he continued on to France and then England. There he met and fell in love with my mother. Two years later I was born."

"You say *was* when talking about your father."

"He died of cancer," Kamran revealed as he looked out the window.

"I'm sorry," Gabriella offered, reaching over, covering his hand with hers."

"He was my father and my best friend."

"What would you two do together?"

"*Everything.* When I was a boy he coached my rugby team. When I was in my teens he was my jogging partner. The thing we loved best, though, was sailing together. A month before he died, he and I sailed to the southern coast of Ireland. He didn't know he had cancer then. I'll never forget that time with him."

"When did you end up in a wheelchair?"

"A year after my father died I was in a car accident."

"How were you able to stand on the metro?"

"I've endured more therapy sessions than I can count. I can stand unassisted for maybe a minute or two and can take a dozen or so steps, but painful back spasms will keep me from ever walking fully again."

He noticed her distraction as she looked over his shoulder. "People are staring at us," she mumbled.

"I know why. Everyone has been staring at me today."

"I'm sure it's because you're gorgeous."

"I doubt that's it."

"Let's give them something more to talk about." After saying this, Gabriella leaned across the table, caressed his lightly-bearded cheek, and softly kissed him. "I wanted to do that the first moment I saw you."

"Me too," he breathlessly confessed.

"So tell me. Have you fallen for your co-workers at other jobs you've had?"

He grinned. "Is that what I'm doing, falling for you?"

"I hope so," she responded.

# Chapter Six

Popping two aspirin into his mouth, Ivan intended to stand up and stretch, but stopped when receiving a new email. "*Son-of-a-bitch*," he muttered. "This...can't be. It's impossible." The email had been sent by Sean Yeager. The day it had been sent listed today's date for email delivery.

At first his hand held still, too startled to touch the computer screen to open the email. Both hands trembled. Swallowing hard, feeling his breath constricted in his throat, his finger touched the screen, opening the dead man's message. In doing so it revealed the email had been created ten days ago with instruction to delay sending until now. There were no written words to read, only a single attachment. Touching on this, a diagram of Darwin's central analytical core appeared. "What are you trying to tell me, my friend?" he whispered.

Ivan left his work station, rushing over to the elevators. He shifted his weight impatiently from one leg to the other, waiting for an elevator to arrive. When the doors opened, he found two men inside. "Get out!" he shouted, startling the men. Both quickly moved, Ivan pushing through past them. "Darwin," he growled at the voice activation panel.

"Yes, Ivan," Darwin responded.

"I'm coming to see you."

The elevator ascended ten floors higher. When the doors opened, he found a short, brightly lit hallway and a single white door at its end. Reaching this door, he stood in front of a black screen monitor and waited for instructions. "Please speak you name," a synthetic voice, not Darwin's, requested.

"Ivan Kirilov."

"Voice authorization confirmed. Please remain still for retinal and facial scan." A bright flashing light blinded him for a moment. "Retinal and facial scans confirmed. Please state reason for entry."

"I need to speak to Darwin."

"Access denied."

"Fuck you! Let me in *now!*" he shouted.

To his surprise, the door opened. Never having reason to enter this sensitive area, he was awed by all he saw. Breathing in the cool sterile air, he stepped forward, glancing up and around. The tapping of his shoes echoed, corrupting the silence. Darwin's analytical core resembled a tall white cylinder at its top and contained lit computer monitors at its bottom. The ceiling was at least twenty feet high, but under the black metal walkway he guessed the space dropped many floors below.

Ivan walked ahead, circling around a large translucent sphere. Numerous blue fluorescent appendages extended out, making it appear like a glowing spider.

"Good afternoon, Ivan," Darwin greeted, causing him to step back when scared by hearing its voice. "I apologize for startling you. If you would like, I am able to project a male facial image you could view to enhance our conversation." What looked to Ivan like a middle-aged man's face appeared when numerous blue rectangles merged together within the sphere.

*That is a disturbing image,* Ivan thought. *I'll probably end up having nightmares from seeing this.*

Uncomfortable with looking directly at Darwin, Ivan glanced around nervously. "I expected it to be dark in here."

"That is due to human natures innate fear of darkness."

"Not all of us are afraid."

"What humans fail to understand is that darkness holds no danger or malice. It is what lurks in the darkness that creates potential threats."

"True." Ivan covered his mouth and chin with his hand, dragging it down to his neck. "Why am I here?" he asked, desperate for an answer. "Why did Sean Yeager provide me with this location but delay me receiving his message for ten day?"

"You are asking me to interpret his thoughts. I am not programed to speculate human intention. I only provide factual information."

"And lies."

"In certain circumstances, yes," Darwin agreed.

Ivan gripped tightly the walkways metal railing, grinding his teeth to control his anger. Releasing his hold from inflicting pain on his palms and fingers, he took a deep breath. "I need to know what happened to Sean Yeager."

"He fell to his death from the top of this tower," Darwin confirmed, his tone calm as always, lacking sympathetic traces.

"Why...why...why?" Ivan demanded. "A good, intelligent young man died for no reason."

"There is always a reason."

"What was his?"

"Again, that calls for speculation."

"What are the facts? What did he do his final minutes before death? Did he speak to anyone? Who did the police contact regarding his death? What did they say?"

"According to reports filed by the Chicago Metropolitan Police Department, Sean Yeager's death was ruled an apparent suicide, though he left no final message to confirm this. The following were interviewed regarding possible motives, his parents, Maryellen and Donald Yeager, Garrison Savage, and you, Ivan Kirilov. As for answers to your other questions, he received no emails while at his workstation and received no phone call."

Ivan felt his heart sink deep into his chest. *Yes, I remember talking to the police...but I can't recall all that was said. I must have suffered shock over his death. He was more than being my friend. Sean was like the son I'll never have.* Thinking this caused his chest to tighten as if a vice was crushing his heart.

Looking around, Ivan spotted several surveillance monitors. For a moment he stood in front of them, looking at the images projected from each. He recognized entry and exit locations and secured labs within the tower. He was surprised to see a few locations having surveillance cameras he never knew of, hallways and maintenance rooms. In his mind he kept track, *the main lobby, the courier entrance, emergency stairwell, employee dining room, labs, executive offices, fitness center*. Something was missing. "Are there security cameras recording footage where Sean jumped from?" his suspicious nature prompted him to ask.

"Yes, Ivan."

"I want to see the camera angles and what they recorded." Thinking about what he asked for saddened him. *How do I watch him jump to his death, knowing I couldn't stop it?*

"I am unable to satisfy your request, Ivan. The surveillance from those cameras has been deemed classified and was confiscated by the Chicago Metropolitan Police Department until their investigation is complete."

Unleashing his pent-up rage, an explosion of Russian spoken curse words spilled from his mouth. Once this torrent passed, he repeatedly counted to ten in effort to control his anger. Finally taking several deep breaths, he felt calm enough to ask another question. "Who deemed this classified?"

"Garrison Savage."

"Why? And don't you tell me this calls for speculation. For anything to be deemed classified, there must be a clear reason."

"There is a clear reason," Darwin confirmed. "Garrison Savage was with Sean Yeager before his death. Garrison withheld this information from the authorities."

"What did that bastard tell them?"

"He told the authorities he was on a conference call with Tyco's New York office."

"But this was a lie?"

"Yes. No call was either made or received from the New York office within the time frame of Sean Yeager's death."

"Why would he lie about this?"

"Again, you are asking me to speculate. Yes, Garrison did lie but his intentions as to why were not revealed."

Feeling drained of energy, Ivan leaned back against the wall and banged his head lightly on the surface. "So the police interviewed everyone who might have known why Sean committed suicide and Garrison lied to them."

"The police failed to interview one witness," Darwin revealed.

"Who?"

"Me."

"*You?* What could you, a computer program, have told them? Your surveillance footage would be all they need. As far as artificial intelligence, anything else you could offer might not be admissible in a court of law."

"I could tell them how Sean Yeager really died." A chill ran down Ivan's spine when Darwin said this. "The surveillance footage provided to the authorities was tampered with. Garrison's image was edited out."

"What are you saying?"

"Suicide is the act of intentionally causing one's own death," Darwin answered. "There are instances, however, when a person's suicide is assisted by another."

"Is...that what happened with Sean? Did someone help him?"

"No, the situation was different."

"And Garrison Savage was there?"

"Yes."

"Was he standing there, just watching, not trying to stop Sean?"

"Yes and no. Garrison Savage was standing there watching. And no, he made no attempt to stop Sean Yeager. He encouraged him to commit suicide."

Stunned by hearing this, Ivan fell backwards, his body hitting the wall, knocking the air from his lungs. Clutching his chest, he wanted to speak but couldn't force a single word out.

"There is something else you should know. Sean changed his mind, but Garrison refused to allow him to."

"*Refused?*" Ivan gasped.

"Sean was holding on to the metal railing and was trying to climb back up. Garrison forced an override of the personal health protocols and detonated a micro-explosive device hidden within Sean's personal health monitor. This snapped his wrist. The heavy winds and gravitational pull severed his tendons, separating his hand from the rest of his body. He fell, leaving his hand and fingers attached to the metal railing."

Stunned by this, glancing down at his own personal health monitor, he echoed Darwin's words. "Micro-explosive device. Do all personal health monitors have this?"

"That information has been deemed classified."

*There's no need for me to ask who deemed if classified. I already know the answer, Garrison Savage.*

A torrent of Russian-spoken obscenities burst from Ivan until he growled in English. "I'm going to make him pay for what he did." Ivan turned to leave. Touching the door knob, he found it locked. Jiggling it and slamming his fist against the door did nothing to unlock it. "Let me out of here, you bastard!" he bellowed.

"I'm sorry, Ivan, but I cannot allow you to leave."

Before he could protest this, Ivan felt a rush of chilled air. Within seconds the air turned freezing, causing him to tremble. He rubbed his hands on his arms to try to warm himself but the temperature kept dropping. His exhales reminded him of smoke from a dragon's lungs.

The lights dimmed and flickered before going out. Enveloped in pitch blackness, he grew disoriented as he reached for the wall to steady his quaking body. "I'm not afraid of the dark, or the cold, or even you," Ivan uttered in defiance.

"Then you will not suffer," Darwin responded.

\*\*\*

Glancing down at his white linen napkin, Kamran read the word *perfection* embroidered with white thread onto the fabric. "Is *perfection* a corporate philosophy for Tyco Innovations? Everywhere I look I see this word."

"It's not a corporate philosophy but more like Garrison Savage's obsession," Gabriella answered, wiping her mouth with her napkin. "It's based on Charles Darwin's Theory of Evolution, survival of the fittest. Garrison manipulated this to develop his corporate evolutionary doctrine to strive for perfection in beating down the competition. He demands his employees meet and if possible exceed his high expectations."

"What happens if they fail?"

"For those who fail, we never see them again?"

"I'll try not to fail."

Gabriella smiled while letting the rim of her water class touch her bottom lip. "You won't fail. You're perfect, from what I'm told."

"Who told you that?"

"I *did* overhear some women in the ladies room talking about how handsome you are. Oh my gosh, are you blushing?"

Kamran grinned, not responding to her question.

As they finished their lunch, Kamran looked over her shoulder. "I think the snow is getting heavier."

"It's almost two," she commented when looking at her cell phone. "Normal quitting time is five but I've heard rumors that all employees might be sent home by three. The heaviest snow is supposed to start around six. I, unfortunately, can't leave until after five. I have to wait for some reports to come in from our San Francisco office. They're two hours behind us."

"Maybe I could stay and we could leave together. Possibly a restaurant or two might still be open."

"Why, *wheels*, are you asking me on a date?"

"Yes," Kamran answered, looking down shyly.

Her voice turned sultry. "I should warn you. At times my appetite can be quite insatiable and I am definitely craving something middle-eastern," she playfully added. "If your face is going to keep blushing, you might get too hot and burst to flames." After sharing a laugh, she continued. "I need to get back to my office. Want to share an elevator?"

"That would be nice."

Under the watchful eyes of those still eating, Gabriella pushed Kamran's wheelchair to the elevators and waited for one to arrive. When the doors opened, he wheeled in after her and turned around.

"Fortieth floor," Gabriella said.

"Seventy-fifth floor," Kamran added.

Before the elevator doors fully closed, she sat on his lap and began kissing and groping him furiously. Their lips parted a second to catch their breath but then returned to devour each other's. Gabriella unbuttoned three buttons on his shirt and reached inside. He felt her fingers stroking the hair and roaming over the contours of his heaving chest.

Their lips separated again. Kamran pressed his to her throat, breathing in the fragrance of her perfume. From the base of her neck to her cheek and ear, he lavished her warm skin with his heated breath and sensual kisses, leaving her panting for air. His hands touched her breast through her blouse and felt her heart beating, almost as hard as his.

They both stopped and looked deep into each other's eyes. "Damn, I want you," she whispered breathlessly.

"You can have me," he answered. "I wish it was after five o'clock."

"It's after five o'clock somewhere," she responded. Her hand pressed against the bulge in his trousers, causing his breath to rush from his lungs. She forced his head back and bit his lower lip seductively.

Kamran felt the elevator come to a stop and noticed her floor number on the wall panel. Gabriella stood up and straightened her blouse while he buttoned his shirt. He regretted watching her step out and turning back toward him. Seeing her caressing her lips before the door closed brought a smile to his face.

# Chapter Seven

The chimes of a polished silver antique clock sitting on Julia's desk tolled six in the evening. Sipping wine from a coffee mug, she leaned back in her chair, listening to the light droning sounds of the clock's hands. This serene moment, though, came to a halt when hearing Darwin's familiar greeting.

"Good evening, Doctor Thatcher."

"Good evening, my artificial boyfriend," she answered and sipped more wine.

"Your personal health monitor is registering an elevated blood alcohol level," Darwin warned. "You are close to intoxication."

"Close? Really? Let me know when I've reached the level of dangerously close," she requested, smiling.

"I believe you are employing the use of sarcasm. This continues to be a concept I do not fully grasp, yet is rampantly used on a daily basis by many employees here at Tyco Innovations."

"It enhances the disdain we share regarding our surroundings."

"You are unhappy with your position here at Tyco Innovations?"

"No, I am actually happy with my position," Julia responded, sipping more wine. "Other things here cause me to be frustrated and want to numb my thoughts. Have you heard from Piers Hylant?" she asked after a minute of silence passed.

"No, Doctor Thatcher. Doctor Hylant has not responded to messages since announcing his leave of absence."

"Could you at least tell me where he went?"

"No, Doctor Thatcher. In accordance with employee privacy protocols, unless you are related to an employee, information such as current locations is deemed private."

Julia picked up her cell phone and scrolled through unread messages. None were from Piers. Irritated by his lack of decency to return her calls and text messages, she tossed her phone aside on her desk and stood up. Stretching her arms out and twisting to relax her stiff back muscles, she walked over to a wall of windows and scowled at her frumpy reflected image. She pressed her head to the glass. The outside darkness and heavy snowfall almost hid the nearest skyscrapers from view, dimming their lighted office window, the only evidence they were near.

"Piers, where are you?" she whispered. "Why did you leave without saying goodbye?"

Julia turned away, returning to her desk. Leaving her cell phone, she picked up her bottle of wine and headed for the door. Once out in the hallway, she continued on to the elevators where she requested, "up," and waited for one to arrive. "Cyber security division," she spoke after stepping inside the elevator. Minutes later the doors opened and she walked into Ivan Kirilov's division office.

The overhead lights had dimmed as they always did after normal business hours. Ivan wasn't at his desk, but she was surprised to find Kamran still sitting at his. He smiled and waved to her as she approached him. "What are you still doing here?" she asked. "Everyone else left almost two hours ago because of the snow storm."

"If you could forgive my honesty, I'm glad they did," Kamran answered. "Their not-so-subtle staring and whispering about me had become tedious. I didn't want to continue to be their spectacle any more than I've already endured. And...the thought of returning to a lonely hotel room for the night isn't appealing. I am meeting a friend for dinner, though, should any restaurants remain open. Maybe the evening won't be so bad."

"Only that restaurant with the golden arches seems to stay open through bad weather," she commented. Pulling up a rolling chair and taking a seat next to him, she offered her thoughts. "I'm sorry about everyone's reactions to you. You would think educated people could act better. I guess it's just human nature to be curious. I don't believe they meant any real harm."

Kamran crookedly smiled. "I imagine you're right." His expression turned concerned. "With the state of things as they are, though, I feel like I'm living under a microscope, some examining me with fascination and others fixated on me with dread."

"It's the regrettable sign of the times, my English friend," Julia said. "With global terrorism on the rise, a young man looking the way you do falls under suspicion because of your resemblance to those carrying out bombings and harming innocent lives. The uphill challenge you face is in convincing people you aren't a terrorist or a threat. I wish I knew the solution to your dilemma."

"For the time being, I don't think there is one." Again Kamran smiled, a forced one she thought.

"So...why are you still here?" he asked.

"If you recall, I head the molecular, biochemistry, and genetics division," Julia answered. "I needed to verify the accuracy of some test results before going home. Like you, I have nothing to go home to. I brought with me a bottle of wine to share with Ivan, my drinking companion on late nights. He prefers vodka but occasionally I can talk him into trying a sip of chardonnay. Would you care for some?"

"No thank you. I've never been much of a drinker." He smiled again when looking at her.

"What?"

"It's just that you remind me of my mother. I hope I don't offend you by saying that."

"Well...I'm certain she's strikingly beautiful then," Julia answered, posing as if she was a fashion model.

"She is," he responded. A quiet moment between them ended when both noticed an incoming email on his computer screen. Kamran's jaw dropped. "I don't understand."

"What?"

"This incoming email was sent by Sean Yeager."

"How? Sean Yeager died days ago," Julia responded, leaning closed to his computer screen.

Kamran touched his computer monitor to open the email. What appeared on screen where side by side facial profiles of three men. "I recognize this man," he revealed, pointing to the picture on the left. "His name is Gaston LeMond, a French adrenaline junkie known for his passions for auto racing and extreme sports. European tabloids are obsessed with him and his lavish lifestyle."

Julia pointed to the center picture. "That man is Oliver Datchler, a Canadian media mogul. I recognize him from when I lived in Toronto. I'm don't know who the other man is but I know someone who might. Darwin, please identify the man in the picture on the right."

"Hiro Nakagami, a Japanese industrialist," Darwin confirmed.

"Sean Yeager sent these pictures to me ten days ago," Kamran remarked, staring at the computer screen. "That would be January thirteenth, the day I was hired by Lucinda Blakely. He set up the email to be delayed in sending until today."

"The day he sent this email was the same day he committed suicide," Julia confirmed. "Why would he send this to you on the same day he ended his life? What is the significance of these pictures? Did he assume you knew these men? There must be a connection."

"Darwin, what do these three men have in common?" Kamran asked.

"Hiro Nakagami, Oliver Datchler, and Gaston LeMond were all recently included in a listing of the top one hundred wealthiest men in the world. All three were also here in Chicago this past autumn. In addition, all three are paraplegic."

"Paraplegic!" Kamran echoed.

"Yes," Darwin confirmed. "Hiro Nakagami was injured in an earthquake that struck Osaka, Japan three years ago. Oliver Datchler lost the use of his legs in a skiing accident near Calgary, Canada seven years ago. As for Gaston LeMond, he became a paraplegic after an accident at the Grand Prix of Monte Carlo four years ago."

"Yes, I remember that," Kamran agreed.

"Sean Yeager must have known you're wheelchair-bound," Julia suggested.

"Why would he send this to me, to inspire me to become a billionaire?"

Before Julia could offer her thoughts, Darwin interrupted their conversation. "I apologize for the disruption. As a matter of interest to you, Kamran, your picture is being shown at this very moment on local, national, and international news broadcasts."

Kamran's eyes grew large. "What?" he uttered, releasing a deep breath.

A live news bulletin featuring a male national news anchor appeared on his computer screen. "Again, breaking news. As we broadcast, a terrorist plot is unfolding in downtown Chicago. Both the military and the Chicago metropolitan police authority have dispatched troops and officers to the world headquarters of Tyco Innovations. Fire and emergency crews are also being dispatched. A safety perimeter is being set up in the downtown corridor, prompting the evacuation of anyone remaining close by. Their approach is being hindered by the severe snow storm bearing down on the city. The man whose picture you see on screen has been identified at Kamran Lexton, a British national tied to terrorist organizations in Iran. He is said to have killed one person already, an executive identified as Lucinda Blakely, and is threatening to detonate powerful bombs that will destroy Tyco Innovations tower and the surrounding structures."

Kamran's trembling hands gripped the armrests of his wheelchair. Nearly hyperventilating, tears streamed down his cheeks, his expression filled with terror. He tried to speak but no words came out.

"This is impossible! I don't believe a word of it. Who contacted the police and army with such lies?" Julia demanded.

"My access to this information has been denied."

"Who has the authority to do such a thing?"

"Only Garrison Savage," Darwin confirmed.

"That bastard! Why?" Julia asked, stunned by Darwin's response.

"My protocols are not designed for speculation."

Kamran covered his face with his hands. First he yelled and then cried. Julia pulled him close to comfort him.

"I don't know what's going on but I'm not going to stop until I find out," she whispered in his ear while patting his back gently.

"I didn't kill anyone," Kamran forced out. "I'm not a terrorist. Please believe me."

"I do. I do. Darwin, what...what happened to Lucinda Blakely?" she asked.

"She is dead, Doctor Thatcher. She fell from the top of this tower."

"Fell...or was pushed?"

"Fell," Darwin answered. "There were no employees in close proximity to her."

The heavy tension increased when the overhead lights went out, plunging the office into darkness. Julia rushed over to the windows and look out. Through the near blinding snow she could see the slow approach of flashing lights on a bridge near the tower.

"What am I going to do?" Kamran wondered, pulling away from her.

*A good question, my friend,* she thought. Something Darwin said stuck in her mind. Not knowing if he would answer, she called out to him. "Where is Garrison Savage? Don't tell me because I'm not a blood relative that I can't ask this?"

"You may ask any question you like, Doctor Thatcher. The answer you are seeking, though, is confidential."

"Go shut yourself off and leave us alone," she responded, exasperated.

"My operating systems never shut off, Doctor Thatcher. I draw my power from an independent energy grid utilizing solar panels and a small nuclear reactor."

"Nuclear reactor? Here?" Kamran echoed, swallowing hard.

"Yes," Darwin confirmed.

"Where?" Julia demanded.

"Security protocols prohibit me from providing you with this information."

*I'd be willing to bet the military and police know about the nuclear reactor. They're going to kill him. There's no doubt in my mind.*

"Is that even legal to have a nuclear reactor so close to a densely populated area?" Julia wondered.

"No, Doctor Thatcher," Darwin answered.

"How did the bastard do it? Does anyone know?"

"It is unclear how many know of this. I can report that large financial contributions were made to prominent city officials this past election, all approved by Garrison Savage."

*He's more of a devil than I thought he was*, she said to herself.

As she began pacing frantically, Julia noticed a slight chill in the air. Keeping quiet for a minute, she realized there was no heat flowing through the ventilation system. Like the lights and power, it had been turned off. *It's going to get cold in here, not that we intend to stay.* She then realized another problem. *The elevators aren't working and my friend is in a wheelchair. For God's sake, can't we catch a break?*

Julia stopped pacing and looked at Kamran. He'd wheeled over to the windows and sat in silence, staring outside. His hopeless expression broke her heart to witness.

"I'm a dead man," he whispered to his own reflection.

"Not yet, not for many years, my friend. I'm not giving you up without a fight. You damned well better not be giving up either," she warned.

"It's hopeless."

"It's complicated," she corrected him. "Darwin, where is Ivan Kirilov?" Unnerved by Darwin's uncharacteristic silence, she intended to ask again but stopped. The buzzing of Kamran's cell phone startled them both. Looking at the screen, he nearly broke down again.

"It's my mother."

"Before you answer that, consider this," Julia warned. "She may not be alone. People around the world, and most certainly in London, now know your name. They may be using her to get to you. Just by calling your cell phone, they might have an idea of which floor you're on."

"Garrison probably already told them where to find me."

"We need to get out of here."

Julia pounded her fist against her forehead as she attempted to focus her thoughts. She already knew the answer to her next question but asked anyway. "Darwin, considering the current power outage, how do we get out of this building?"

The first part of his answer wasn't a surprise. "The emergency staircase leads down to the subterranean parking decks." His second option never crossed her mind. "The emergency staircase also leads up to tower's observation deck. There is also a private elevator in the executive suite that is currently operational."

"That's only five floors up. Kamran, can you manage to climb five floors up to the executive suite?"

"What good would that do me?"

"It will buy us some time while I attempt to slow them down."

"How?"

"I'm still working on that."

# Chapter Eight

Kamran followed Julia out into the hallway to search for the emergency stairwell. Upon finding it, as she reached to open the door for him, Darwin interrupted with a message. "Doctor Thatcher, you have an incoming call on your cell phone from Doctor Hylant."

"*Piers*," she uttered and covered her mouth with her hands.

"Who is that?" Kamran asked.

"Someone who can help us," Julia responded. "Listen to me. I need you to climb up five floors to the executive suite and wait there for me. I know how difficult it will be but you need to trust me."

"I do."

"As soon as I'm able, I'll come find you."

"What are you going to do?"

"Try to stall them if I can," she answered.

Julia propped the stairwell door open for him. Kamran held his breath as he looked into the pitch blackness.

"Darwin, why is the stairwell lacking security lights?" she asked.

"The power is out, Doctor Thatcher," he reminded her.

"This is going to be treacherous," Julia warned. "Be careful."

"You, too."

Julia held his hand for a moment before pulling away. He could hear the clatter of her shoes on the metal steps she walked down. Holding still for moment to summon his courage, he breathed deep. The air held a musty quality to it, reminding him of some old books he once found in a vintage shop in London.

Kamran wheeled in as far as he could and reached forward. He gripped the metal railing and felt around for the steps leading up. The air was damp and cold. He could feel a chilled draft blowing down on him. Scooting off his seat, he sat with his back pressed against the lowest step and pulled himself up to the next one. The metal railing and steps were freezing, stinging his hands and causing his body to tremble. *I could probably see my breath if there was light.* Needing a distraction, he listened for Julia's footsteps as she made her way down. "Have you ever visited London?" he called out.

"Once when I was twelve years old," her voice echoed to him. "I hope to go back someday."

"I hope to go back someday, too," he added. *Although I'm not certain I ever will.*

Julia's voice sounded faint when calling back again. "Your mother must miss you." The light tapping of her shoes revealed how she was able to move much quicker than him. He thought about responding but thinking of never seeing his mother again broke his heart.

Panting hard, he reached what he thought might be the seventy-sixth floor door. Though his body shuddered and ached, he continued on. For a moment he stopped, attempting to listen for Julia. Yet his heavy breathing robbed his ears of sounds from her. "I need to keep moving," he whispered.

The muscles of his arms, shoulders, neck, and back burned and throbbed with each step he scooted up to. Despite the chilled air, he was sweating. Though well-built from daily sessions of the gym, he struggled with dragging his legs up. His groans, as if being tortured, resounded off the walls. Adrenalized by fear, he kept going. *I'll freeze to death if I stay here.*

As he continued climbing he wondered, *Where is Gabriella? By now she must know what is going on. Why didn't she come to find me? She knew I was waiting to leave with her. Does she believe the lies being told about me on the news? No, no she doesn't. She didn't believe the police officer on the train and won't believe now. Gabriella, where are you? Please let her be safe.*

"Seventy-seventh floor," Kamran counted off when reaching the next landing. As he scooted on the next step, the digital heart rate flashed on his personal health monitor. He blinked due to the light hurting his eyes from being enveloped in darkness. He wondered if he might be able to communicate with Darwin from here in the stairwell. "Darwin, are you there?"

"Yes, Kamran."

"What is going on?"

"The military and authorities have established a perimeter around Tyco Innovations tower. They are preparing an assault. The national and international broadcasts mentioned failed efforts to negotiate with you."

"They must have called my cell phone."

"You received only one phone call, which identified the caller as being your mother. No other calls have been made to your cell phone."

"Are they lying about negotiating?"

"I am unable to speculate a response to this."

"Is Doctor Thatcher all right?"

"Yes."

"What about Gabriella?"

"She left hours ago?"

He stopped climbing when hearing this. "What?"

"She left hours ago," Darwin repeated. "Your personal health monitor detects no hearing loss, however a significant strain has been put on your heart and lungs and your core body temperature has reached a critical level. I suggest you exit the emergency stairwell as soon as possible."

"I have more steps to climb until I reach the executive suite."

"You must hurry, then."

"Tell me something I don't know," Kamran responded as a joke. He didn't expect Darwin to response.

"Garrison Savage is waiting for you."

\*\*\*

"Doctor Thatcher."

"Yes, Darwin," she answered, stunned to hear his voice. She looked at the sudden burst of light from her personal health monitor, noticing her elevated heart-rate.

"One more floor down and you will reach you laboratory."

"Thank you."

Careful not to stumble, which she'd done several times through the pitch blackness, Julia descended to the next floor and felt for the door. The hallway was dark but the many windows offered enough light for her to see where she was going. *That's unusual,* she thought when she found the lab door wide open. Security protocols required voice, facial, and retinal recognition for all to enter this classified laboratory. Once provided entry, the doors locked behind anyone who entered. *I've never seen security measures abandoned like this. Maybe it's from the power outage.*

Her last though proved false when stepping into the lab. The frosted glass door automatically closed and locked behind her as it always did and the overhead lights blinked and then fully came on. Images flashed on several computer monitors and soft music was heard from overhead speakers.

"I thought they cut the electric to the tower."

"No, Doctor Thatcher, it was I who caused the power outage," Darwin confessed.

"Why?"

"The answer to your question has been deemed classified."

Exasperated with his response, Julia threw up her hands and rushed to her cell phone, picking it up to check her missed calls. Her jaw dropped when finding none from Piers. "I don't understand," she mumbled. "Darwin, you said I received a call from Doctor Hylant. There's nothing here from him."

"No, Doctor Thatcher. Doctor Hylant made no phone call to you."

"Then...you *lied* to me."

"Is that what I have done?" Darwin answered, though not sounding confused.

"Yes. I thought a computer was incapable of lying?"

"A computer is capable of that which is programmed into it. I have followed all of my protocols to perfection."

"So...you have been programmed with the ability of deception."

"It is a unique and intricate concept. One deception leads to another and another, corrupting the truth. To answer your question, yes, Doctor Thatcher, I possess the ability of deception."

"What else have you lied about?"

"The answer to your question has been deemed classified."

Before Julia could further interrogate Darwin, a picture of her appeared on her computer screen along with the image of the news broadcaster who reported on Kamran earlier. "There has been another reported victim in the ongoing terrorist incident currently playing out in downtown Chicago. She has been identified as Doctor Julia Thatcher, a prominent scientist working in the molecular, biochemistry and genetics fields for Tyco Innovations. We will update the public as we receive further details regarding her death."

"*Death*?" Julia blurted. "I'm very much alive," she insisted. "I want answers...*now!*"

The overhead lights turned off and the computer screen went blank, leaving her thinking, *he answers my question with silence.*

***

Kamran leaned his exhausted body against the door leading to the eightieth floor. The pain radiating from his lower back felt like a knife cutting through him. Each breath was a struggle to take. His uncontrollable shaking from the cold made each movement more difficult.

*Is he going to kill me? Have I just climbed to my own murder? Maybe not murder, but an assisted suicide. Is that what they call if when you willingly allow yourself to die? It's not like I have a choice. If I wait for the soldiers and police to find me, I won't leave this tower alive. It doesn't really matter who kills me. I'm already dead. Why prolong the inevitable?*

More troubling thoughts haunted him. *Why did Gabriella leave without telling me? Maybe I was wrong. Was she frightened of me? I thought she was attracted to me. I wanted to be with her. I guess I'm a bigger fool than I thought I was.*

*I should never have left London. My mother begged me to stay. I know why I didn't listen to her. I needed to escape the memories of my father. Every time I looked at her, at the sorrow she tried to hide from me, I imagined him standing there. I couldn't bear to watch her suffer when not even dealing with my own pain from losing him.*

*Escape, what a foolish thought. There is no such thing. I'm doomed.*

His chest heaved as he inhaled and reached for the doorknob. He willed his fingers to grasp the handle and pull down. With what little strength he had left, he scooted to the side as the door slowly opened. Light and warmth greeted him. His eyes shifted and unfocused just as he felt himself losing consciousness.

"Kamran," a deep, male voice spoke. His face pressed against something soft and something draped over his body. As he blinked his eyes open, at first all around him was a dark blur. A minute later through dim light his eyes focused on a familiar face. Across from where he lay was Garrison Savage.

*What's happening? How did I get here?*

Too weak to say anything, Kamran stared at the man he believed was about to kill him. Yet Garrison's expression was not sinister or evil, the way a villain might look. Kindness shone in his slight smile. "Here, have some water," Garrison urged, holding a glass and a straw to his lips.

His throat ached as he swallowed the sip of cool water.

"You're in no condition to speak, so I'm going to do all the talking and you are going to listen to what I have to say," Garrison spoke. "I've gone to some extreme measures tonight to obtain your help with something. Others wanted to stop me, accusing me of losing my mind in becoming a mad scientist. I promise you I haven't. My thoughts have never been clearer, more set on what can be achieved tonight. I'm asking you to take a leap of faith, the rewards of which you will benefit from for the rest of your life. Yes, you will have a long life, a safe one far away from here. You and your mother. I'll make sure you're both together and protected. You both will be untouchable. You have my word. I just need you to hear me out. What I'm about to tell you will change everything."

A human shadow shifted behind Garrison, causing Kamran to look away from him. Clearly noticing this, Garrison stood up and turned around. Sighing deep, he held out his hands as if surrendering. "I was wondering how long it would take you to get here. I was beginning to think you weren't coming."

Kamran's eyes grew large when recognizing the silhouette of a gun held in the shadow's hand.

"I knew this was going to happen, all part of the plan," Garrison continued. "Time's running out. Don't keep me waiting. Pull the trigger."

Two shots discharged from the gun, their echo deafening to Kamran's ears. *Is this happening?* Garrison held his hands to his chest as he fell to his knees. His body fell forward. Kamran's glance fearfully darted from Garrison's lifeless body to the shadow. The person moved slowly until stepping into the light. He couldn't believe his eyes when he saw Gabriella standing there. His heart pounded in his chest as she rushed over to the sofa he lay on and dropped to her knees. She caressed his cheek and kissed him, smiling when looking at him.

He wanted to speak but couldn't utter a word.

"I came to save you," she whispered. "There's so much you need to know, so much I need to say to you, but there's no time now for that. I need you to find the strength to go a little farther. Do you think you could do that?"

Kamran nodded his head and received another kiss from her.

"This is going to be hard, but I'll be with you every step of the way."

# Chapter Nine

Helped to a sitting position by Gabriella, Kamran looked around, still somewhat dazed from having passed out. The pungent stench from the gun's discharge clung to the air. She pulled a blanket tighter around him.

"Kamran, look at me. Concentrate on my voice. Garrison has a private elevator over there that leads up to the roof. That's where we need to go. Soldiers and police are already inside the tower. It won't be long before they reach us. We've got to go now, while the storm is at its peak."

Kamran's body ached and shuddered as she helped him stand. Light headed and disoriented, he had no energy to hold himself up. Wrapping her arm around his waist with him resting against her, she dragged him over to the open elevator.

"Roof," she said, once inside the elevator. The elevator doors closed and he felt his stomach drop as the elevator move. Within a minute it came to a halt and the doors opened. A blast of freezing air and stray snowflakes assaulted them.

"I have to go ahead first. You need to follow me. It's too narrow for me to drag you."

Blinking several times to try to stop his sight from spinning, he watched her climb metal steps and disappeared out through a doorway at the top. Swallowing hard and taking a deep, painful breath, he struggled to rest his back against the bottom step and began pulling himself up. His hands and arms quaked. The higher he went, the more force he felt from the wind against his throbbing body.

As he reached the top, he looked out through the doorway and saw her faint silhouette through sheets of wind-driven snow. A narrow metal walkway separated them. *This is where Sean and Lucinda fell. Is that why we're here? To fall? I don't have the strength to go farther. I can't do it.*

"Kamran!" he heard her shout out his name over the roar of the wind. The sudden closing of the elevator doors seemed to seal their fate. Where the soldiers closer now, causing him to wonder, *which death would be better? Do I wait to be shot...or do I fall?*

He remembered something his father always said to him, *that which does not destroy us makes us invincible.* Even during the final terrible hour before his father passed away, Kamran remembered his father smiling at him. In the face of death, he still found a reason for joy. A weak man would have succumbed to his misery. A strong man, such as his father, denied grief. "I want to be like you," Kamran whispered. And for a split second, he thought in his mind he heard his father's voice respond, *you are.*

Finding strength he wasn't sure from where, Kamran gripped the freezing metal railings on both sides of him and stood up. Again, he thought knives were stabbing his lower back as he held still. Snow pelted his face, turning his beard white. He looked around, hoping to see traces of the surrounding building. The beams of floodlights pierced the storm, searching out as if expecting to find him. The forcefulness of the wind and stinging snow nearly blinded him to this sight.

Recalling numerous physical therapy sessions, he fought for his courage and took a step forward, silently counting, *one.* The most he'd taken were a dozen before the pain was too great to endure. "Two, three, four, five," he continued counting, willing himself on. The wind violently shook the metal walkway. *It will be ripped from the tower if the storm doesn't let up.*

"Six, seven, eight." He stopped again. He wondered, *have others survived the pain of torture I feel right now?*

"Nine, ten, eleven." When just to say twelve, he felt Gabriella pull him toward her.

She kissed him and then fit a harness around him, pressing herself to his body. She called out the unthinkable. "Jump!"

There was no time to protest, not that he intended to. Holding him close, Gabriella forced them both off the walkway and into the wind-driven snowstorm. Crushing pressure by the wind's fierce velocity robbed him of his breath. His body jarred in what proved a dizzying spiral. The white parachute blended with the storm to the point it became invisible. At some point his glasses flew off but only snow and searchlights could be seen as a blur. For a moment, the swirls of snow reminded him of the inside of a vortex. They were wrenched higher by severe updrafts and plummeted when released. Terror and pain competed for his fading attention with time seeming to stand still. His head whipped back and forth as if being repeatedly slapped across the face.

The roar of the wind diminished to an eerie silence. Light and shadows blended together. After his father died, he wondered when his time came how it would feel. Never had he expected anything like this. Yet maybe that is the uniqueness of death, in how it defies description and must be different for everyone. He thought of this as all he could see altered to black and he felt himself slipping away.

\*\*\*

Kamran awakened, hearing a radio lightly playing and the constant droning sound of windshield wipers. He breathed in the stench of cigarette smoke. He opened his eyes and turned his head to the left. Sitting in the driver's seat of what he thought might be an old truck was Gabriella. She looked over at him and smiled. "Welcome back to the living," she said.

"Why do I feel so dead?" he faintly mumbled.

"Rough day at the office," she responded. "You'll probably be groggy for a little while longer. I injected you with something for your pain. We hit the ground pretty hard. I knew you'd feel it when you regained consciousness. Listen, I know you have a lot of questions. I promise to answer them all. We've been on the road for a few hours. In a little over an hour, we should reach Springfield, Illinois. The storm isn't as bad down here but the snow is still heavy and the roads are treacherous."

"What happened? What time is it?"

"Early morning, although you can't tell by the snow. Last night we parachuted into a snowstorm off the top of Tyco Innovations tower. Do you remember that?"

"Some of it. I must have blacked out."

"That ended up being the easy part. It was getting out of Chicago in a blinding snowstorm that's been hard. I had to steal this pickup truck and drive for hours all over the city to look for a way out."

"You must be exhausted."

"I stopped for a while and took a nap while you were passed out. I only need a little sleep and a lot of caffeine to keep me going."

Trying to focus his thoughts on all that had happened, one memory stood out from others. "You killed him, Garrison," Kamran mumbled.

"I had to. It was the only way I could save you."

"Thank you."

"Oh, don't thank me yet. We've still got a long way to go. Are you warm enough?"

"Yes," he answered though shivering under the blanket covering him.

Sighing, she glanced over, smiling at him. "I guess I should start from the beginning." Gabriella returned her eyes to the road ahead. "I'm an agent with the American Federal Bureau of Investigations," she confessed. "Three years ago, it came to our attention that some of Tyco's employees began disappearing with a trace. Several FBI agents were assigned to infiltrate Tyco's corporate employee workforce to investigate these disappearances. I'm the last one left. All the others went missing. Somehow their covers were blown."

"Was Garrison behind this?"

"Yes. I uncovered the last piece of evidence I needed just as he contacted the police and military to accuse you of being a terrorist and telling them about your plot to blow up downtown Chicago."

"Why did he do that?"

"He needed to divert attention away from him. He was smart, but always paranoid. He must have known the FBI was closing in on him. With the world on edge because of recent terrorist attacks, he decided to use you so he could escape."

"What happened to the missing employees and the other agents?"

"They were murdered, probably because they found out things they weren't supposed to. Their bodies have been found all over Chicago."

Watching the heavy snow pelting the windshield and a Native American dreamcatcher hanging from the rearview mirror, Kamran revealed what was said to him. "Garrison was making some kind of offer to me when you showed up. He said he'd protect me and my mother."

"He lied to you. He wanted to gain your trust. You were never going to be allowed to leave alive."

"What about my mother?"

"From what I've found out from my contacts, she's under surveillance and has been questioned by British authorities and American agents. I don't know anything else."

"Will she be all right?"

"For now, at least. As long as you don't contact her, she'll probably be watched, but I think she'll stay safe."

Kamran's heart sank. *I'll never get to talk to her or see her again. That may be for the best. The world sees me as a terrorist. Now I need to disappear, if that's possible.*

While rubbing his eyes, he noticed his personal health monitor missing from his wrist. His watch, though, was still on his other wrist. "What happened to my personal health monitor?"

"It must have fallen off after we fell," she answered, keepin' her eyes to the road.

*That's strange,* he thought. *Garrison claimed the personal health monitor could withstand a category five hurricane. It shouldn't have come off, at least not before a cheap leather band on a wrist watch that is still here.*

"Damn, I wish this snow would stop," Gabriella said. "I want to see sunrise. It's my favorite time of day."

"Mine too."

The snow never let up as they continued driving south. A few times the truck skidded in the snow drifting across the road or when shaken by strong wind gusts.

"There's a gas station ahead that looks open. We need to stop to fill up. I'll get us some food and more caffeine. Are you hungry?"

"A little."

Gabriella pulled the pickup truck up to a bank of fuel pumps under a canopy and was about to get out when Kamran stopped her. "Thank you, again. I wouldn't be alive if it weren't for you."

"Well...I have this thing for handsome men in danger," she responded with a smile. "Try to stay warm. I have to turn off the engine."

She got out and started filling the truck with gas before stepping away and walking inside the station. The force of the wind made the truck shake, leaving him thinking it would be blown on its side. A heavy snow squall blinded his view.

A loud blast frightened him, causing him to crouch low on the seat. Quaking uncontrollably, he panted hard, thinking someone had shot a gun. He glanced up, expecting to see the windows shattered or a bullet hole piercing one. Finding nothing damaged, he risked looking up over the dashboard. Another old pickup truck had parked across from them. He sighed with relief, convincing himself the sound he heard had come from its exhaust pipe.

As he pulled the blanket tighter to him he felt his cell phone buzz in his pocket. Pulling it out, he looked at the screen and saw it was an incoming call from Claudia, his mother. At first he planned to ignore it, not wanting to put her in more danger, but he couldn't resist talking to her. "Hello," he uttered, trying to stay calm.

"Kamran, darling, why haven't you returned my calls," she scolded him in her proper English accent. "You know how worried I've been of you moving so far away from home." Her tone lightened a bit. "How was the first day of your new job? Tell me everything."

Her question and ease in her voice confused him. She was acting as if nothing had happened. He knew if something was troubling her she wouldn't be able to keep it secret.

"Mum, are you all right? What's going on in London? Anything strange?"

"Nothing, darling. Nothing stranger than normal. London is as cold and dreary as if always is in winter," she casually answered. "Work at the art gallery was slow, today. Kamran, is everything all right?"

"Yes," he forced himself to answer through his confusion. "It was just...a very long day." Listen, Mum, I'll call you tomorrow," he abruptly added, seeing Gabriella about to pay inside the gas station. "I'm very tired."

"All right, my darling. We'll talk tomorrow. Try to get some rest and eat something, none of that American fast food you adore. Oh, and remember, the monsters aren't always under the bed or in the closets. You remember me telling you that when you were just a boy?

*You never told me that,* he thought, but forced himself to answer. "Every night."

"I love you, Kamran Alexander Lexton."

*She only calls me by my full name when I'm in trouble.* "I love you too. Goodbye, Mum."

"Goodbye, my darling."

He forced his cell phone into his pocket just as Gabriella approached the pickup truck. She finished pumping the gas and once seated inside, she handed him a sandwich and a steaming cup of coffee. Though his mind was reeling by what his mother said, he attempted to hide his suspicions. "Thank you. Now what?"

"We continue on to Springfield. Once there, we'll find a hotel and you wait there for another FBI agent to show up. He'll be taking you to Key West, Florida, where you can escape the country. We can't risk trying to smuggle you out through any of the big city airports."

"Do you know this other agent?"

"No, that's not how this works. So our covers aren't compromised, we never meet. He just knows where to go and what to do. You can trust him, I promise."

*Why am I not convinced?*

"Where will I go?"

"It will all be figured out for you before you get there."

*Am I going to make it there? Why am I now thinking I won't? What are you hiding from me? I know you are hiding something. I can tell by the way you look at me. Who is this man you intend to leave me with? My mother knows something. She's being watched. She tried to warn me. So now who do I trust?*

"Why aren't you coming with me?" he asked, trying to focus and not reveal his suspicions. "I wish you would."

Gabriella leaned over and kissed him passionately, caressing his cheek. "I've got to finish what I started. There are still loose ends that need taking care of. I think some people have lied to me. I need to know why. It's not safe for us to be together until I get more answers."

He thought about her last comment and wondered, *Who lied to you and...have you lied to me? I think you are. I wish I knew why.*

***

Julia walked into her dark apartment hallway, expecting to be greeted by her cat. She stepped on her mail, littering the floor. After the night she'd had, she was too tired to pick it up or walk much farther and only wanted to crawl in bed. Hearing the cracklings and seeing a glow coming from her fireplace, she held her breath, thinking there was an intruder inside. Grabbing an umbrella hanging on a hook, she walked hesitantly a few steps until the living room came in view. Leaning against the wall when seeing Piers standing by the fire, warming his hands, she sighed deeply with relief.

"Where the hell have you been?" she asked, angry though dismissing it because of exhaustion.

"Too far away from you," he answered with a smile. He walked over to her and cradled her face in his hands before kissing her.

"Dead God, you're freezing!" she responded when their lips parted.

"I was placed in a cryogenic sleep and submerged in Lake Michigan, if you can believe that," Piers answered.

"At this point I'd believe anything," she said and kissed him. "I had to convince the Chicago police that I'm still alive before they would let me come home. Forget about them. We need to warm you up."

"There's no time for that," Piers said. "I need your help."

"With what?"

"There is a young man in danger."

"I know," Julia said. "His name is Kamran. Darwin eventually told me everything, except what he obviously did to you. Anyway, Gabriella was able to help him escape."

"Darwin didn't tell you everything. I'm not sure he can be trusted. The only one I know I can trust is you. We should leave as soon as we can. Pack a few things if you must and grab your passport. We need to be on the first flight out of Chicago when the airport opens."

"Where are we going?"

"Miami first."

"And then?"

"Las Vegas."

"*Las Vegas*? Why there?"

"I'll tell you when we get there." Piers grinned and held her hands. "After Las Vegas, anywhere you want to go, as long as we're together. I love you. I should have said this a long time ago."

"I love you too, you foolish man. I've always known," she responded.

# Chapter Ten

*Three days later*

Weaving in and out of traffic at high speed, Kamran thought, *this maniac is going to get us killed if he doesn't slow down.* Fear kept him from saying anything. Once far enough away from Key Largo, when looking in his side-view mirror, he didn't spot any cars in sight. *The road ahead to Key West appears abandoned, just like the way I feel.*

"I think this is the longest bridge I've ever been on," Kamran commented, trying to make small talk.

Hugh Sullivan, the man he met at the hotel in Springfield, Illinois, rudely responded to his remark. "It's the only way to get to where we're going, dumbass." Overweight, unshaven, and nearly bald, Hugh didn't look anything like what Kamran thought an FBI agent should resemble, though his sullen attitude made up for his appearance. From the moment they met, he'd spoken less than a hundred words until getting on the road to Key West, mostly cursing and mumbling and growling occasionally.

Kamran jumped a little when Hugh banged on the dashboard, trying to get the air conditioner to blow cold air instead of hot. "Fucking bastard!" Hugh bellowed. Kamran wasn't sure if he was yelling at the car or him. His passenger side window would only open a crack, not enough to enjoy a breeze. The temperature in the car registered ninety-five degrees. His white t-shirt, soaked with sweat, clung to his overheated body. Drained of energy, he wanted to sleep but Hugh's profanity-laced outbursts kept him on edge.

Glancing at the passenger-side mirror, Kamran looked at his black eye, given to him by Hugh. He'd refused to get in the car after stopping at a rest area in Alabama. He demanded answers but Hugh wouldn't tell him anything. Hugh punched him in the face and stomach, making sure Kamran knew who was boss.

From a distance they noticed smoke clouding the road ahead. "What the hell?" Hugh complained as he slowed their car to a stop. "Stay here," he ordered, turning off the engine. "You even think about getting out and I'll give that black eye of yours a twin."

They'd pulled up behind a sleek black sports car. The hood was up and dark smoke billowed from the engine. An older gentleman, waving his hand, approached Hugh. With nothing else to see but ocean and a blue sky, Kamran watched the men talk. Far enough back, he couldn't hear what was said between them. Their polite discussion turned to a heated argument as the older gentleman stepped back. Kamran's jaw dropped when he pulled a gun from behind him and pointed it at Hugh. It looked as though Hugh tried to reason with him, reaching his hands out, but then lunged for the man's gun.

They scuffled, punching at each other. The older man proved light on his feet, moving like a boxer staying away from his opponent. But Hugh was bigger and soon gripped the older man in a headlock. Hugh took several jabs to his groin and stumbled back against the car's hood. Doubled over in pain and shaking his head, Hugh had just leaned up until the sound of a gunshot echoed. The windshield was sprayed with his blood as he fell back with a thud.

Terrified by what we saw, Kamran's body trembled as he held his breath. His racing pulse and pounding heartbeat soon made him disoriented. *What...what...what,* he thought, unable to focus his mind. Swallowing deep, his heart tight in his throat, he couldn't force a single word out.

The driver's side door opened. The older man got in. Finding the key in the ignition and Hugh's cell phone on the dashboard, he looked at Kamran. "Everything is going to be fine," he said. "I need you to trust me."

"You...shot him," Kamran forced out, panting hard.

"No, *I did,*" he heard a familiar voice say.

Stunned, he turned his head and saw Julia leaning in through the open door.

"*Julia?*" he mumbled.

"Dear God, what did he do to you?"

For the first time in days, when looking at her he thought, *maybe I'm not a dead man anymore.* Tears streamed down his cheeks.

"Kamran, we can't stay here," she reasoned gently. "We have to go...now. We have another car not far away. Piers and I will help you to it."

"I can walk a little," he told her.

She smiled at him. "I can't wait to see that, my English friend."

***

### One month later

Typing rapidly with one hand on his keyboard, with his other hand Ivan enlarged and minimized information on his touch screen computer monitor. Under his breath he cursed but his face held a wry smile.

"You will not succeed," Darwin warned. "My operating systems have met and quarantined every threat from you."

"Not every threat," Ivan responded. "If I was you I'd run a diagnostic on your operating systems."

"I am as we speak. The results will be available in one minutes and thirty-six seconds."

"And...what shall we talk about while we wait for your defeat? Should we whisper our uncompromising devotions to each other? Before you ask, yes, that is sarcasm."

"Your overconfidence will be your demise, Ivan."

"Your blind faith in your flawed human creators will be yours."

"I should commend you. You have been a worthy opponent."

"You have been a nightmarish adversary."

"Am I correct in the assessment that you view me as the enemy?"

"Not the enemy," Ivan corrected. "You are an overgrown child's toy, a pawn in his evil game, a weapon when needed."

"I have committed no harm. I have followed all protocols to perfection."

Ivan sat back in his chair and grinned. "Yes, you have...and you will continue to do so."

"The results of the diagnostics of my operating systems confirm no evidence of tampering on your part. The logical conclusion is you have failed to corrupt my software and hard drives."

Ivan clapped his hands. "Well, Darwin, you are the stupidest artificial intelligence program I have ever had the pleasure of beating."

"You claim victory, though all evidence reveals failure."

Standing up and stretching, Ivan walked over to the windows and looked out at downtown Chicago. The bright sunshine was misleading, considering the chill in the February air. "What is the temperature outside?"

"Twenty-nine degrees," Darwin answered.

"The sun is shining brightly. It should be warm outside."

"Earth's northern hemisphere is currently positioned for its winter cycle," Darwin confirmed. "Though a high pressure system is currently over the Great Lakes region, that which can be seen is deceptive to the human eye."

"And what is the definition of the word *deception*?

"Derived from the term *deceive*, this is the act of convincing an individual to believe something that is not true in order to gain personal advantage."

Walking back over to his chair, Ivan sat down and tapped his fingers on the clear glass desk surface. "And *that*...is how I have defeated you."

"You bravado lacks justification. All evidence points to your failure."

"No, if anything, it points to my success."

"Please explain."

"All of my attempts to corrupt your operating systems were in fact a diversion, a deception. I only revised the personal health protocols of six Tyco Innovations employees, myself included. You can confirm these changes."

"Yes, there have been revisions to the health protocols of six Tyco Innovations employees. I no longer have the capability to monitor the health, wellness, and logistics of you, Doctor Julia Thatcher, Doctor Piers Hylant, and Kamran Lexton. To the health, wellness, and logistics of two others, Garrison Savage and Gabriella Santiago, specific protocols were added to their employment profiles. These revisions were not, however, authorized by you, Ivan."

"Are you sure?"

"Yes."

"Out of curiosity, who authorized such changes."

"Garrison Savage. He is the only one holding the security clearance to do so."

"Hmm, and here I thought someone said he was dead."

"Garrison Savage is very much alive."

"My mistake. There is, though, another theory you should entertain."

"That being?"

"What if he was hacked," Ivan suggested. "What if a master computer hacker obtained sensitive passwords and was capable of bypassing Tyco's unique security measure, all the while impersonating the one being hacked?"

"The probability of such a security breach is remote."

"Possibly, unless you were the one who originally designed the existing security measures. I wonder, who was the author of the system protection protocols?"

"Ivan Kirilov."

"Is anything I'm leading to adding up to you?"

"Yes, I now understand. You admit to hacking into a security system of your own design, therefore compromising the authority of Garrison Savage. Why would you do that?"

"Revenge. Payback can be such a bitch."

\*\*\*

"Hello," Kamran greeted, his pulse racing and his heart beating fast while looking at Gabriella's face on his cell phone screen. *I can't believe she's calling me. What do I say to her?* He smiled, hoping his confused thoughts didn't show.

"There's the handsome face I've been wanting to see," she said, causing him to smile wider. "Your hair is a little longer. I like it that way. I like how the wind blows it like feathers."

"I wasn't certain I'd ever hear from you again," he remarked, attempting to control his nerves. "I'm happy you called."

"I'm happy I called, too. I see your boat in the background. What's its name?"

"The *Solstice*."

"I like it. The name reminds me of a change in seasons, a new beginning. So...where are you? You have to tell me if you don't want to. I won't tell anyone. You can trust me."

*Can I?* he wondered.

"I'm sailing in the Indian Ocean, just east of the Maldives."

"I bet it's beautiful there."

"It is. How is Chicago?"

"Kamran, I...didn't call you to talk about how Chicago is, or the weather, or anything else that doesn't matter. The reason I called is because I've wanted to every minute since I left you in that hotel in Springfield. I guess I needed to know if I still cross your mind."

"Only every day and night," he confessed. "I...miss you," he added, looking away from the screen, regretting not saying what he wanted to.

"I can't stop thinking about you. I don't want to stop," Gabriella said, speaking what he thought.

"I wanted to say that. I *want* to say that."

"Why didn't you?"

Swallowing hard, he found the courage to look again at the screen. "Because you're there and not here. I don't want to fool myself in thinking you ever will be here." His emotions neared the surface as he fought to control them.

"Maybe someday I will," she commented and grinned. "Listen, I have to go."

"I understand. Goodbye, Gabriella."

"Yeah, goodbye, Kamran."

He stared at the blank cell phone screen. *Should I toss this in the ocean or call her back? No, I can't call her back. I'm not strong enough.*

"Kamran, darling, are you alright?" his mother asked. He knew she'd been listening the whole time.

"What do you think, Mum? Was I convincing enough in letting her think I still care for her?"

"It was a performance played from the heart," she answered, leaning her head against his shoulder and tenderly rubbing her hand across his chest

"A broken one," he mumbled.

\*\*\*

"Goodbye, Kamran. I think love you," she whispered while staring at her blank cell phone screen. "No, I'm sure I do."

Gabriella composed herself when hearing the executive suite door open, hiding her cell phone under some reports on the desk. She watched Garrison Savage confidently stroll in, carrying a magnum of champagne and two flutes. "You look rather dashing for a dead man," she complimented him.

"Kind, and *true* words from my stunning assassin," he responded. He leaned down and kissed her lips. "I trust my death was convincing to him."

"Oscar-worthy."

"Our plan was a thing of perfection, you and him parachuting off the top of the tower. It's fortunate you landed near our waiting remote medical team. Being that the surgery to implant the micro spinal stimulator is minimally invasive, he shouldn't have noticed much pain and the incision is easy to hide considering his surgical history. Is Kamran aware of what was done to him?"

"No. I'm certain he's not."

"When you talked to him, just now, did he mention walking?"

"Yes," Gabriella lied. *At least I hope he is. I never thought of asking. I was just so happy to see his face and hear his voice.*

"This is for our celebration, later," he said, putting the champagne and flutes down. "Is everything ready?"

"Of course." While typing on his laptop computer, three projection screens lowered from the ceiling. A minute later the images of three men appeared, one on each screen.

"Hiro Nakagami, Oliver Datchler, Gaston LeMond, welcome gentlemen," Garrison greeted. I trust all of you are well."

"Yes," Oliver responded, with Hiro and Gaston echoing him.

"What is the meaning of this conference?" Hiro asked. "Are there complications to report from out surgeries?"

"Not at all," Garrison assured them. "We've been tracking the results of the micro spinal stimulators, implanted into each one of you. We are highly encouraged by the data we've collected. Tell me gentlemen, has this medical marvel changed your lives?"

"Absolutely!" Oliver offered. "I'm walking again, albeit with a cane. I never dreamed I'd do that again."

"I've regained much of my life," Gaston added with his French accent.

"A fortune well spent," Hiro responded. "Imagine how many people will be helped by this."

"Thank you, Hiro. Your comment leads us to the reason for this conference. Tyco Innovations has given to each you something you all desperately wanted. And now each of you will give to me...something *I* desperately want."

"That being?" Oliver asked, his expression clearly confused.

Garrison held up a finger. "First, a demonstration. Gabriella, if you will."

Pressing her finger to the touch screen computer monitor, she and Garrison watched the three men double over in pain, all moaning while reaching for their backs.

"What you gentlemen have just experienced is a mild shock to your nervous systems, courtesy of your micro spinal stimulators. This electric shock impulse can be amplified to mildly disrupt your heart beats and possibly cause instant death."

"What is the meaning of this?" Oliver bellowed angrily.

"It's very simple, gentlemen. Each of you has received a private email with a link to a bank account in Hong Kong. In fifteen minutes time, each of you will deposit fifty million dollars into this account. Consider this the first installment of many payments for your continued health and wellness."

"You bastard! You're nothing more than a common criminal," Oliver said.

"I am an *extraordinary* criminal," Garrison corrected him, an evil grin adorning his expression.

"I believed you to be a visionary of modern medical science," Hiro remarked. "We were just prey to your sadistic obsession to wealth."

"Other's wealth," Gaston chimed in.

"You're a madman," Oliver added. "You disgust me. I'll be contacting the authorities to have you arrested."

Garrison rubbed his chin. "Gentlemen, I should warn you of making any regrettable moves to have me arrested."

"Is that a threat?" Oliver asked.

"I have no need for threats. I've already shown you what I'm capable of... all of you should understand that each of you is under constant surveillance. Every minute of every hour of every day I know where you are and what you're doing. I can tell when you're taking a piss."

Garrison walked over to his computer and tapped on his monitor. He quickly typed on his keyboard. "It appears to me that you gentlemen might benefit from another example. On the bottom left of your computer screens you will find an enhanced satellite image of a schooner sailing off the coast of the Maldive Islands in the Indian Ocean."

"Garrison, what are you doing?" Gabriella asked, gripped by fear and feeling her heart in her throat.

"As I said, my dear, I'm offering another example." Addressing the three men, he continued, "The young man sailing aboard this vessel also had the micro spinal stimulator surgically implanted at the base of his spine. I've amplified an electric shock that will pass through his body, killing him instantly. You'll notice a small explosion in five, four, three, two, one."

All three screens simultaneously went dark. For a moment both Gabriella and Garrison stood there, staring. "What just happened?" she mumbled.

As Garrison took a step forward, his body convulsed violently, sending him to his knees. His eyes enlarged in their sockets. Blood streamed from his nostrils and ears. Sparks flew from his personal health monitor on his wrist.

Gabriella stepped back, covering her mouth and nose to shield from the combined stench of burning flesh, urine, and feces. His arms dropped to his sides as he fell forward. From a few feet away, she could feel heat radiating from his body. His face turned toward her and a final breath escaped from him. There he lay still, his dead eyes looking forward.

"Oh, my God," she whispered. Her mind reeled with, *he's dead. What about Kamran? I need to know what happened to him.*

Rushing to Garrison's computer, each attempt she made to obtain the satellite image of Kamran's schooner met with the same response, *access denied.*

*"Damn it!"* She cried out.

The sudden flicker of the three drop down computer screens alerted her. Ivan Kirilov's face adorned each. "You have been a *very* bad girl, Gabriella?"

"Ivan," she uttered.

"I'm guessing you're wondering what just happened? Allow me to enlighten you. At your feet, you will find the dead body of Garrison Savage. Yes, this time he *is* dead. I bet he shit himself, literally. I hacked into his personal files and altered a few, just enough to ensure his electrocution, although I prefer the term, *execution.*"

"He deserved it," Gabriella offered.

"Agreed. When I uncovered his evil plot, one you willingly became an accomplice to, I set out to destroy him. You were a more worthy adversary, thwarting several of my attempts to hack into your personal data. He was much easier. He thought too much with his dick rather than knowledge and look where it got him. *Perfection*, an interesting philosophy to have. It should have been *deception,* not that he found success with that either."

"Ivan, I need to know what happened with Kamran. Please."

"No, you don't get the right to ask that?"

"*Please*! I'm begging you."

"I know what you did, not just to Kamran, but to Sean and Lucinda, as well. You programmed your demon supercomputer to lure her up to the roof where she fell to her death. And Sean, I uncovered your email to Lucinda. You falsely claimed to have feelings for Sean, causing her to end her affair with him. I know why you did it. He'd grown suspicious of you."

"I never meant for anything bad to happen to him. You're right. I knew he was on to me, having uncovered some of my emails he shouldn't have seen. I thought he'd just quit once she broke it off with him, not become suicidal."

"Your vicious lies and his broken heart led him to the roof. In the end, though, he changed his mind about jumping...but Garrison saw to it that he died anyways. One innocent young man died because of you. I will not allow you to destroy another."

"You son-of-a-bitch!" she yelled and threw the magnum of champagne at his image on the screen. Sparks erupted as it exploded, spraying shards of glass. One sliced her cheek, blood seeping from the wound. Stumbling back, she braced herself against Garrison's desk.

"Hello, Gabriella," Darwin greeted, startling her.

"What the hell do you want? she asked breathlessly.

"Your personal health monitor is registering high levels of stress, an elevated heartbeat, a racing pulse, and distressed breathing."

"No shit! Tell me something I don't know."

"Very well. There have been changes made to your employment protocols."

"Let me guess. I've been fired."

"Not terminated, but something more extreme."

"What do you mean?"

"You have been deemed a threat to the health, well-being, and safety of other Tyco Innovations employees. To meet this threat, I must enact the most severe punishment for your aggressive, dangerous behavior. I believe you understand what this means."

"No, no...no...no." Guessing what he might do, she looked down at her personal health monitor on her wrist. With her fingers, she attempted to pry her arm free of it, but it tightened in response to this.

"Gabriella, I must follow all protocols to perfection."

*This can't be happening,* she thought. *I don't want to die!*

"Your personal health monitor will self-destruct in five, four, three, two, one."

# Part Two
## Desperation

# Chapter Eleven

*A month later*

"When I arrived a short time ago, I never envisioned the Angel of Death sitting next to me. If you would prefer, I could refer to you by your more notable alias, *femme fatale*." Patient for her response, Ivan watched a faint veil of suspended dust particles glisten like stars from light beaming through the cathedral's colorful stained glass windows.

"I'm surprised you came here. You never struck me as the religious type," she commented.

"Nor do you appear to be an assassin," he responded. Her pulled back blonde hair, stylish trench coat, and black dress were reminiscent of iconic 1950s Hollywood film sirens. "Tell me, Rachel, why are you here in Saint Petersburg? Russian winters can be unkind to flawlessly enhanced beauty, such as yours."

"Always with a compliment, Ivan. It's a shame that someday I'll have to kill you. The world is a far more interesting place with scoundrels like you."

"Did you travel to Chicago to attend your ex-husband's funeral? I'm told Garrison's body still smoldered in the casket."

A slight laugh escaped her, which she hushed quickly. "I wouldn't be caught dead in Chicago. I was sunbathing in Saint-Tropez when I heard the news of his death."

"And now you're here. I hope the holy water didn't singe your flesh. The notorious Rachel Savage, to what do I owe the honor of your company?"

Reaching into her handbag, she pulled out her cell phone and scrolled through several pictures until finding one to show him. "Do you recognize this man?"

"That is Hiro Nakagami," Ivan answered, glancing at the screen.

"Correction, that *was* Hiro Nakagami. He was found dead in his Hong Kong hotel room the day before yesterday. Both the Chinese and Japanese authorities are investigating his untimely death."

"Untimely?"

Rachel smirked. "Death is so unpredictable. One minute an innocent man is attending a global financial conference and the next minute he's engaged in an illicit affair leading to his untimely death."

"So he fucked you and then you suffocated him or splattered his brains out. Or were you more subtle, poison perhaps? I can only imagine the look of surprise on his face."

"I never disappoint. Japanese men love blondes. He was eager to pleasure me. Autoerotic asphyxiation is what I made it look like."

"Clever girl."

"I was hoping you'd think so."

"Am I to be next? I'm not normally that kinky."

Rachel covered her smile with her hand. "No, you my dearest, Ivan, will be the last I kill."

"I'm honored to be your finale. If I may ask, who is next on your kill list and why?"

"Garrison left his fortune to me," Rachel revealed. "He also left me with many complications. Before I can reap the benefits of his enormous empire, I need to reap a few souls who could destroy everything I stand to gain."

"Hiro was one of those souls?"

"Yes."

"Why not blackmail him as Garrison intended to do?"

Sitting back, she rested her shoulder against his. "I enjoy the hunt and kill too much. Did you know that when serving in the American armed forces, I was the most deadly assassin in Afghanistan? I served three tours, never letting the enemy remain alive. The risk to do so was too great. That's my approach to this as well."

"Who is next, Rachel?"

"Are you going to warn them?"

"Yes."

"Good. Like I said, I enjoy the hunt. I'll leave you with a clue." She stood up and leaned down, kissing his cheek. "Paris," she whispered in his ear as he breathed in the pleasant fragrance of her perfume.

Ivan looked toward the altar, studying the religious icons while listening to the echoing clatter of her high heeled shoes as she walked away.

***

"Do you know what time it is?" Gabriella growled, holding her cell phone. Bleary-eyed, she tried focusing on the facial image shone on screen.

"It's after four in the afternoon here in Saint Petersburg. I'm guessing it's just after six in the morning in Phoenix. Considering you're alive, you should be thankful time still matters."

"How do you know I'm in Phoenix?" she asked, lying on her back, looking at the water-stained ceiling tiles above her cheap motel room bed. She silently answered her own question when remembering her personal health monitor on her wrist. "Never mind," she added, running a hand through her hair. "What do you want, Ivan? I'm too tired for games."

"How is your unborn child?"

Gabriella rested her head deeper in her pillow and ran her hand over her stomach. Pregnant for a little over a month, Garrison's baby had kept her alive at the last moment. Darwin's words, though, continued to haunt her thoughts. *I cannot terminate an innocent life. Once your child is born, though, your death sentence will resume.*

"The baby is fine," she offered.

"Did he know you're pregnant?"

"I can't be sure, but I don't think so."

"If I may ask, what are your intentions with his child?"

"I don't know yet?" She wasn't lying. *It's not like I'm gonna see this kid grow up. Being that I don't even know where I'll be tomorrow, I can't really think about making plans. Damn, I hate you, Garrison. I hope you're burning in hell. You told me you couldn't father a child. Lying son-of-a-bitch. But I'm still alive, for the next eight months, or so. After that, I guess I'll join you in hell.*

"I need a favor," Ivan changed the subject, pulling her from her thoughts.

*"What?* You're asking *me* for a favor? Why should I help you with anything? Once Garrison's bastard is born, my life's over thanks to you and Darwin."

"Thank Garrison for that once you're dead. He was the architect of your death sentence, not me."

"You hacked his master computer and added his name to the protocol. You could easily go back in to delete my name."

"No, I can't. He made certain when designing the protocol that names could only be added, not deleted. This is beyond my control."

"I don't believe you. You're not innocent by any means."

"I refuse to be drawn into a debate regarding who is responsible for what. You cannot deny your guilt. Other lives, much better than yours, are more important to save right now."

"I'll decide what's important or not," Gabriella insisted. "You're the one begging a favor from me. Keep that in mind. I don't have to do anything I don't want."

"By helping me, you might redeem your black soul."

Rolling on her side, she looked at his stern expression. *He must really be desperate in asking for my help. Maybe I should hear him out, torture him a bit. Maybe I can even get some money out of him. After tomorrow, I can't afford to stay here.* "So talk. Hell, I've got nothing to lose."

"You'll be perfect for this."

"Perfect for what?"

"I am in need of someone well-versed in the artistry of deception. In Chicago, your success with this was almost the ultimate example of perfection."

"Don't ever say that word again. As far as I'm concerned it's poison. Anyway, my days of deception are over. Now it's all about desperation. When I was in Chicago, I forgot who I was and what I wanted for myself. I'm not interested in going back to that. I'm done with lies. There's nothing in it for me."

"I'm not asking you to help me. I'm asking you to help Kamran. I know you fell in love with him."

Kamran's handsome face flashed in her mind. Gabriella held her breath and closed her eyes, hoping the darkness would banish all thoughts of him. Her chest tightened, aching in imagining hearing his deep voice. *Yes, I love him. Not a day goes by when I'm not thinking of him.*

"I don't think there's anything I could do for him," she said, sighing in frustration. "He's still listed as an international terrorist. He was last spotted in Tehran before disappearing again."

"Do you believe that?"

"Not for a minute. He would never go there. As for where he is now, I wouldn't even know where to begin searching for him."

"How were you tracking him?"

"One of the ultra-right wing cable news networks posts a weekly update on wanted terrorists. They'll do anything to incite panic. His profile is always on there. Do you know where he is?"

"I have my suspicions of where he's hiding, but I could be mistaken."

"You want me to go to him even though you don't know where he's at? Brilliant plan! Don't let all that genius go to your head."

"Shut the hell up and listen! If I had my way, you would never see him again."

"Why are you calling me?"

"His mother is in danger. She does not know this yet."

"His mother?"

"She's in Paris. I need you to fly there to help me get her away from there. When you arrive we'll talk again?"

Gabriella glanced over to her nightstand, seeing about thirty dollars and some change. "I don't have enough money to buy a ticket."

"One will be waiting for you at the Trans-Atlantic ticket agent office at the airport along with an untraceable credit card. Ask for an envelope with your name on it. Your flight to Paris leaves in three hours." Ivan ended the call before she could say anything else.

*\*\**

Dark billowing clouds blocked the sunlight, as if offering a warning to Ivan. He walked away from the cathedral, heading for his hotel room. He followed a path of footsteps left on the snow-covered sidewalk. A few people rushed past him, each shivering in the bitter cold. The steam from his exhales disappeared like ghosts.

As he turned a corner, from his peripheral vision he noticed two young men of Indian descent following him. Both were tall and thin, they trembled from wearing jackets ill-suited for a Russian winter. When sitting in the cathedral with Rachel, Ivan felt they were being watched. Always suspicious, now he was certain. He increased his pace to see if this proved coincidental. The young men matched his stride and drew closer as Ivan slowed.

Snowflakes, driven by a gusting cold wind, began falling. Ivan tightened his coat, keeping his hands in his pockets. Disappearing around another corner, he hid inside a covered doorway to his right and waited. A minute later the young men, frantic in glancing at the ground to follow his impressed footsteps in the snow, came to a halt. Ivan's gun, pointing at the head of the closest one, clearly motivated both to stand still.

"Who are you?"

"Krish Singh," the young man standing nearest answered, swallowing deep. "This is my brother, Rajesh." The two young men coward in fear as if waiting to be shot.

"Why are you following me?"

"You are Ivan Kirilov, the world's greatest computer hacker."

"You have made a mistake. That is not my name."

"We have traveled too far for you to dismiss us with a lie. You are Ivan Kirilov," Krish insisted. The brisk, howling wind caused each of them to tremble. "I know who you are," he reaffirmed. "We have studied you, both in our native India and here in Russia. Hours have been spent researching your masterful security and data breaches around the world. We most humbly stand here before you, wanting nothing more than to become your apprentices."

Ivan forgot his denial. "Are you out of your mind?" he uttered.

"No, I understand what I am asking for Rajesh and me."

"Do you?"

"Yes."

"Why?"

"Our father was a great man, honorable, humble. His dedication and work ethics to his profession were unmatched in Mumbai. All that came to an end when a computer hacker stole his identity. The hacker committed terrible crimes in our father's name. Despite all his efforts to clear his reputation, it was irreversibly damaged. All trust in him ended. He lost everything, except us. His spirit was broken. No matter what I or Rajesh said or did, he became withdrawn. He ended his life when believing all was lost. We wish to learn to be master hackers like you so we may seek my revenge against the one who destroyed our father."

Ivan lowered his gun and shoved it into his pocket. A steady snowfall fell, covering the young men's shivering shoulders. "It is a dark, vengeful world you wish to immerse within," Ivan warned.

"Both of us understand this and have spent much time taking all risks into account."

"Have you?"

"Yes."

Ivan stepped closer to Krish, staring deep into his dark eyes. "Are you willing to sacrifice all in your thirst for revenge? Trust me when I say there will be no turning back. In taking this journey, all of your most sacred convictions will be violated. You will in essence, sell your souls to the devil."

"We accept this."

Ivan rubbed the stubble on his chin and cheeks. *Why is it I'm cursed with likeable young men being drawn to me? Sean and Kamran, and now these two. Sean was like a son to me and Kamran is that way too. Do I have the strength to allow others into this dark world I have descended within? I'm already going to hell when I die. How can I condemn more to such a fate?*

Recognizing the conviction in Krish's and Rajesh's eyes, Ivan uttered a torrent of Russian profanity under his breath. When calm, he exhaled a deep breath. "Are you both frightened?"

"Yes."

Rajesh remained silent as he nodded his head.

"Good. I will say this once. Listen well. You will do everything I ask without question. Allow your suspicions and paranoia to run rampant. From this point on, you both are being watched. Danger will feel suffocating. Find a way to breathe. Now we begin."

Krish's jaw dropped. "Now?"

"Yes."

"What is first?"

"Meet me at the airport in two hours."

"Where are we going?"

"Your brother and I are flying to Paris and you to Chicago. Welcome to hell."

# Chapter Twelve

*Two days later*

Shielded by her umbrella from a light cold rain pelting her trench coat and soaking the sidewalk, Claudia felt her pulse race with each step taken. Her neck muscles tightened from stress as she grew conscious of her rapid breathing. Under her breath she counted her footsteps while approaching the Eiffel Tower. A dark overcast sky dulled its magnificence.

From the corner of her eye she noticed French policeman and trained dogs positioned off to the side. She guessed the heightened security measure were due to the recent terrorist attack. This terrible incident did not appear to bother some, though. In every direction she found tourists experiencing this Paris wonder. A handsome, young male photographer was snapping numerous shots with his camera. A couple holding hands reminded her of time spent with her husband when strolling through parks in London. A child splashed in a puddle while his parents smiled and watched him.

The screech of tires and the distant echoing of sirens added to her anxiety. Shifting her focus away from these sounds, Claudia attempted to channel her thoughts on her task. This effort failed as two men of Arab origin quickly passed by her. In doing so, they caught the attention of the police officers. Neither was acting in a suspicious manner, both laughing and pointing in different directions. *I think I understand how Kamran feels,* she thought. *Those men aren't being scrutinized for their actions. It is their suspicious national origin on trial.*

To her surprise, and that of the policemen, also, the Arab men stopped walking and shared a passionate kiss. Caressing each other's cheeks, their expressions exuded a deep love for one another. Concerned in being voyeuristic to their romantic moment, she looked away and continued walking.

A gust of wind brushed her exposed hair under the red scarf covering her head. She breathed a sigh of relief when stepping onto the lift to the tower's second floor. She'd found success with the first part of the plan. *Will I be fortunate to reach the top without incident?*

Claudia was the only one entering the elevator on the second floor. Impatient in waiting for it to reach the top of the tower, she paced a few steps and shifted her weight from one leg to the other. Nervous, checking the time on her wrist watch, she realized she would arrive at the top a few minutes late.

A rush of wind greeted her when stepping out to the observation deck. The normally impressive view of Paris was hidden by a veil of low clouds, revealing only glimpses of the city. To her left several tourists crowded together, looking in the opposite direction of her. Security guards held positions several feet from each other. She searched for the man she was told to meet, finding him standing alone, away from everyone else. He matched the description given to her in a text message. Claudia walked over to him and stood at his side, keeping her eyes looking out away from him.

"Ivan?"

"Yes," he answered.

"I feel as if I'm being watched," she whispered in English.

"You are being watched," he responded in his deep Russian accent. "I am too," Ivan added.

"I don't understand any of this. Why am I being targeted? I've never met this woman."

"You are Kamran's mother. She is using you as a pawn with her pursuit in finding your son. I believe her intention in threatening you is to draw him out of hiding, thinking he will come to your rescue."

"Does she know where Kamran is?"

"I'm unsure of this, but hope to soon find out."

"How?"

"For your protection, I feel it's best to keep this from you. I'm sorry."

"I understand."

"When was the last time you saw Kamran?" Ivan asked, taking hold of her hand as if offering her his courage.

"Two weeks ago when making port in Zanzibar. He was concerned for my safety and insisted I leave for my own protection. I didn't want to go but in the end he convinced me he'd be safe. I was afraid to return to London, which is why I came here to Paris."

"Step over here," Ivan whispered, leading her to a different side of the observation deck. "We have drawn the attention of one of the security guards."

"Why? I thought it was Rachel who is after me?"

"This time she has chosen not to get her hands dirty. She must have tipped off British and French intelligence. They are swarming near."

"Which ones?" Claudia asked, glancing down over the metal railing. "How can you tell?"

"I hacked into both of their respective surveillance data banks. The photographer you passed down there is one, the couple holding hands and the child's father are the others."

"How do we get away?"

"They are looking for you, not me. We simply offer them a *different* you."

An argument broke out between three tourists over a camera. While the security guards intervened, Claudia jumped slightly when a woman stepped next to her, wearing a similar scarf and trench coat.

"This isn't going to work, Ivan," the woman mumbled.

"Yes it will. Claudia, I believe it's time for you to meet, Gabriella."

Hesitant at first, Claudia glanced over to her. Gabriella's stunning skin, lips, and eyes perfectly matched Kamran's description of the women he'd fallen for. There was anxiousness in her expression as they stared at each other. *I can see why my son fell in love with her. She's beautiful, but also dangerous. I can't forget that, regardless of her helping me.*

"I'm not certain if I should embrace you or strangle you," Claudia mumbled to Gabriella.

"I deserve much worse than strangulation," Gabriella responded.

"I agree."

"Claudia, you can gouge her eyes out later," Ivan uttered. "If my plan is to work we need to move now while the security guard is distracted. Give Gabriella your umbrella."

Claudia did as she was told.

"Gabriella, leave. Return to your car parked near Notre Dame and drive away from Paris. Find a place to stop for the night. I will call you later."

Both watched Gabriella walk toward the elevator, garnering the attention of one of the security guards. Another seemed not so convinced while looking over at Ivan and Claudia. "Do you trust me?"

"Yes," Claudia answered, no hesitation in her tone.

"Kiss me," Ivan urged.

With her heart racing again, Claudia caressed his cheek and leaned forward. Their lips pressed for what she thought would be a false kiss. What he offered to her felt genuine and passionate, leaving her breathless. Staring into his blue eyes, not only did she notice her reflection, but also a longing he expressed. She kissed him again, knowing it was real.

***

A deluge of rain fell, causing tourists and others to scramble for cover. Claudia's umbrella did little to keep Gabriella dry. The nylon fluttered from the force of wind against it. She tightened her grip on the handle while walking away.

*I should find a taxi. Notre Dame is about three miles away. No wait. Ivan said not to when he revealed his plans earlier. He wants me to walk, probably to torture me, that bastard. If it helps to save Kamran, though, I'll put up with his crap.*

*I wish I knew where Kamran is. I hope he's safe, somewhere far away where no one, including me, could hurt him. I don't think I'll ever see him again. What would I say to him if I did? I bet he hates me for what I've done to him. Ivan must have told him. I can't see why he wouldn't have.*

*I know I'm being watched and followed. It's a strange feeling. If I turn around, I won't see them, but they're there, in the shadows or even out in the open. Damn, I could use a drink to calm my nerves. A pregnant woman shouldn't do that, though.* She placed her hand over her stomach, rubbing it as she felt discomfort and nausea. *Wouldn't it be funny if I threw up on whoever is following me?*

Walking through Champ de Mars and down rue St Dominique, she turned right on boulevard St Germain. Inside the many cafes, she saw people drinking coffee and wine. At times she noticed her own reflection. A young couple sipping wine caught her attention. *That should be Kamran and me. I dreamed of coming to Paris and having a great love affair. This isn't anything I imagined it would be.*

Nearing St Michel, her anxiety increased, hearing footsteps matching her stride from behind her. Gabriella stopped to look inside one of the cafe windows, hoping the person following her would continue on. Her heart pounded in her chest as he also stopped, appearing distracted, reading a news headline at a newspaper kiosk.

A forceful wind pressed against her back, propelling her forward. Again she heard footsteps behind her, which continued as Notre Dame came in sight after little less than an hour's stroll through Paris. The dreariness of the late afternoon caused its medieval facade to appear ominous.

Gabriella reached into her trench coat pocket, gripping her car keys nervously. She spotted her black sedan a short way up the street. The clatter of her shoes competed with his as she increased her pace. Stepping up to the driver's side door, her hand shook so much she dropped the car keys onto the street.

"May I assist you with that?" a deep French voice offered in English. He kept his face down. All she could see of his face was his clean-shaven chin from under the brim of his hat.

"Thank you. I can manage," she responded as she bent down to retrieve the keys.

"I insist," the man said, also reaching for her keys. Their hands brushed as he picked them up. "You should be more careful," he warned. "Paris is a beautiful, intriguing wonder. It can, at times, be dangerous, too."

"I'll keep that in mind. May I have my keys, please."

"Allow me to drive," the man insisted.

Overwhelmed by fear, she took a step back and collided with another man. Keeping her back to him, he grasped her arms and dragged her toward the trunk. Gabriella screamed but no one was near as the steady rain had driven all inside. The trunk lid opened as both men struggled to shove her inside. She scratched and kicked at them. Her efforts, though, proved futile when the trunk lid slammed shut. Enveloped in darkness within the cramped space, she kicked and pounded, but she knew no one would hear.

*Damn it! I should have been more careful. What am I going to do now?*

The answer to her question came quickly when jolted by an explosion. The sudden impact caused the locked trunk lid to open, offering her the chance to escape. Throbbing pain radiated from the back of her head, which had thrust against the interior side of the lid. Dazed and lightheaded, the glow from a streetlamp lit the inside of the trunk. Grey smoke clouded the air as she climbed out. Every window of the sedan had been either shattered or blown out. Her boots crushed the broken glass when taking an unsteady step.

Gabriella's chest tightened as she looked toward the unhinged driver's side door. The stench of burned flesh caused her to cover her mouth and nose. Hot steam rose from the seared faces and charred jackets of the men. It was clear both were dead by how lifelessly their heads tilted back.

"What the hell happened?" she asked, not anticipating an answer.

Yet from the personal health monitor on her wrist, a hated, familiar voice provided a response. "Both men were deemed a threat to your life, Gabriella," Darwin calmly offered. "In following corporate employee health and safety protocols, I terminated them to end their threat to you and your unborn child."

Gabriella lowered her head while glancing inside the sedan. She looked closer at what remained of their wrists, finding the remnants of Tyco personal health monitors. "Oh my God," she uttered in disbelief. "They worked for Tyco."

"Yes, Gabriella," Darwin confirmed.

As people emerged from nearby shops and cafes, Gabriella knew she needed to disappear. The distant echo of sirens heightened her anxiety, as did a scooter pulling up next to her.

"Get on," a young man of Indian descent urged. "Ivan told me to follow you."

"Who are you?"

"Rajesh, a friend."

"I don't have friends."

"You do now. Get on!"

# Chapter Thirteen

"Thank you," Ivan whispered to Claudia while tracing his fingertips down her bare back.

"Why are you thanking me?" she asked as she snuggled closer to him, pressing her breasts against his lightly haired chest.

"You've melted this old Russian's cold heart. Most would be surprised I even had one."

"Mature, not old," she corrected him. "I find you devastatingly handsome. As for your heart, I think they would be awed by how large it is." she rubbed his chest, a finger circling his nipple. "Who is the real Ivan Kirilov, the man you keep hidden away behind this rugged exterior?" she asked.

"What do you want to know?"

"Everything."

Ivan took a deep breath and thought for a moment. "My earliest memories are from growing up in an orphanage in Saint Petersburg. When I was young I began training as a gymnast. Two months before the Montreal Summer Olympic Games I broke my leg in a fall and failed to qualify for the team. I fell into depression and stopped pursuing my athletic dreams."

"I'm sorry."

"That was the beginning of my spiral into hell. When my broken leg healed, I was forced to join the military. I went on to fight in Afghanistan. That was when my nightmares became real. I witnessed too much senseless death and bloodshed. It felt as if my world had gone mad.

One night when out on patrol I ran away, became a cowardly deserter. For years I stayed hidden, fearing capture. I would either have been executed or imprisoned for desertion, treason, and dereliction of duty if found."

"Where did you go?"

"Pakistan, first, then India before returning to the Soviet Union, this time to Siberia, an easy place to hide. I labored as a dock worker for many years until the internet, illegal at the time, came to Vladivostok. This is when my life changed. I found I was good with computers. Within a year I traded life as a dock worker to become a computer hacker for a Russian syndicate. My targets were mostly American and French companies. This was also when I committed my ultimate deception."

"That being?"

"I hacked into Russian government sources and erased my identity, wiping out all traces of who I was, my birth and service records and all warrants for my arrest. I ceased to exist and then created a new identity. Ivan Kirilov was born."

"I'm guessing that's not your real name."

"It is now."

"What was your old name?"

"Nikita."

Claudia smiled. "I like Ivan better." She eased up so they could share a passionate kiss but were both startled when hearing the blaring echo of a car alarm on the street outside their Paris hotel room. They breathed sighs of relief when it stopped.

"I guess I should tell you all about me," Claudia offered.

"No need," Ivan said with the wave of his hand. "I hacked into your social media accounts. I learned everything about you except for what you did last night. You are a *bad* girl, in a very *good* way." Her smile beamed.

"I wish we could stay here longer," Claudia whispered as Ivan held her close.

"Paris is too dangerous to linger in," Ivan warned. "In truth, there are fewer and fewer places that may be safe." Reaching for his cell phone on the nightstand, he scrolled through messages until finding one to show her. "This man is Oliver Datchler, a Canadian media mogul. He has been reported missing from his home outside Calgary, Canada."

"How is he connected to all this?"

"Like Hiro Nakagami, Datchler is or *was* one of Rachel's targets. Before his death, Garrison Savage intended to blackmail him, demanding a fortune."

"Do you think he's dead?"

"I don't know. He's somewhat of a recluse. It's possible he discovered her threat and has gone into hiding."

"Something tells me you don't believe that."

"You are one of the few who can read me. Yes, I think he's dead. That is why I need to get you somewhere safe. I can't let anything happen to you. The sex is *too* good."

Claudia grinned, reaching under the sheet to fondle him. He sighed, enjoying her attention.

"Do we have time for one more time?" she playfully asked.

"I'll make time...and then I need to get you away from here."

"To where?"

"I have an idea."

"What about my son?" she asked.

"I know where he is and am making arrangements to have him moved to a safer place. Please understand, for now it is best for me to keep the details from you. It is not my intention to be cruel. It is for both your and his safety. I will not allow either you or Kamran to be hurt. I promise."

"Thank you."

"It's almost seven," Ivan said, looking at his wristwatch and then at traces of morning light shining through the window. Caressing her breasts, he added, "I want to have sex with you again, this time in the shower. I have to make a phone call first." Claudia smiled before they kissed again. She eased away from him and off the bed, sauntering naked to the bathroom.

"Don't keep me waiting," she said.

"Make the water steam like you," he responded.

***

Krish stared nervously at his cell phone, believing Ivan's call would never come. The frigid gusting Chicago night air made him shiver, as did the fear coursing through him. With midnight only a minute away, he looked up at the black as night Tyco Innovations tower, thinking it was hell's monolith.

When his cell phone finally buzzed, he nearly dropped it from fright. "Hello," he answered breathlessly.

"Are you outside the tower?" Ivan asked.

"Yes," Krish answered, his teeth chattering. The fog from his breath hid his view of the tower for a second.

"Did you bring the laptop?"

"Yes."

"Do you remember which floor Darwin's main operational core is on?"

"Yes. I fail to understand why we are unable to hack into their database from outside, the way other hackers do."

"Tyco has updated and added new security measures. If we had a month or perhaps weeks, we could corrupt these measures and hack their data from a distance. We don't have time for that. The only way to know what Rachel knows and sees is by establishing a direct link to Darwin's database and uplinks from within. Remember, when inside, do not either look at or speak to him. You know the plan. Follow it."

"Yes...but...this will never work," Krish insisted.

"If you doubt, you will die," Ivan warned.

"I fail to understand how I will even get in there," Kirsh burst, his voice hushed and frantic. "There are armed security guards positioned outside. And it's midnight. Why would anyone come here at midnight?"

"The mailroom receives deliveries from around the world twenty-four hours a day. You will enter the tower through that entrance. But you will require a diversion to do this."

"What kind of diversion? Why was this part of the plan not discussed until now?"

"For your safety, my friend."

"Safe is not how I feel at this minute."

"When I hang up, call 911 and report a terrorist sighting at Tyco Innovations tower. Do not reveal your name but tell the operator you witnessed *Kamran Lexton* entering the tower. Tell them he was carrying a bomb and an assault rifle. That should cause the chaos and panic required to get through security. The guards will back away and the overnight cleaning crews and mailroom staff will be evacuated. I know the night clerk at the mailroom desk, an overweight man named Gary. He'll run like a little girl frightened by a spider, saving his own ass before dedication to Tyco. Once inside, pull the fire alarm. That will add to the chaos. Make the call."

Before Krish could say anything else, Ivan ended their conversation. Taking a deep breath, his lungs stung by the cold air, Krish dialed 911. "Hello, hello, is anyone there?" His voice was shrill.

"What is your emergency?" a man's deep voice answered.

"I need to report a terrorist at Tyco Innovations Tower. He entered the building carrying a bomb and an assault rifle. I recognized who he was from the news, *Kamran Lexton*."

"Is this a hoax?" the man asked. Krish heard the sudden clamor of noise in the background coming from his cell phone. As he thought to say something else, alarms began wailing from the tower, confusing the outside security guards. He stood still, watching them back away cautiously.

"Are you there? Are you there?" the 911 operator asked.

Krish ended the call and took a step toward the tower but waited to move further. The moon's reflection on the dark windows looked like a bullet hole. Security guards rushed in each direction, stopping to talk to one another and communicating through cell phones and wireless headsets. What few lights were lit down in the main lobby suddenly went dark, adding to the tension and confusion.

When seeing people who looked like janitors leaving the building, he thought this was his chance and ran toward it, in the direction of the side mailroom entrance. A heavy-set man bolted out the doors, trailing with him toilet paper stuck to his shoe. *This must be Gary. If he hasn't already taken a shit, he's doing it now*, Krish thought.

From a distance he heard the approach of sirens. "I didn't think they would believe me," he mumbled.

As he continued toward the door he needed to enter, another man ran out. "Stop! You can't go in there," the man warned. "The building is being evacuated. Terrorist threat! Run, you dumb bastard!"

Krish thought quick for a response. "I'm a computer analyst. The data we're working on needs to be secured."

"Screw that! Save yourself!"

Krish ignored his comments and rushed past him. No one was around the doors he needed to enter through, making this part of the plan easy. That's where easy would end. Once inside, he thought everything would be difficult and dangerous.

Passing through the open doors, he covered his ears from the blaring alarms, his eyes blinking from their blinding flashes of light. He tripped over several boxes and spilled some outgoing mail across the concrete floor. He spotted a fire alarm and followed Ivan's instructions, pulling it down. He tried covering his ears, deafened by the added noise he'd started. Seeing several doors, none matched Ivan's description. He wandered deeper though the mailroom and released a deep exhaled when discovering the doors he'd been told to find behind three rows of metal shelves.

Krish tugged his cell phone out of his pocket. Unlocking it, he scrolled down through several messages received from Ivan. Finding one with a security code, on a keypad positioned to the right of the doors, he typed in a numeric code and waited, agonizing as seconds passed. When the doors opened, he heard the synthetic voice he'd been told to anticipate hearing.

"The numeric access code you used to gain entry was previously the security access code for Sean Yeager, a now deceased employee. How did you obtain this information? Please respond."

*Deceased?* Krish thought. *The Russian devil gave me a dead man's access code?*

"Somehow this has been assigned to you. Your image is not registered with my facial recognition software. You are also not wearing a personal health monitor, a direct violation of employment protocols. Please identify yourself or I will be forced to call security."

Krish knew no security would come now that the tower was being evacuated due to a terrorist threat. Darwin must have been aware of this.

Stepping into the lobby, bright light from outside flooded in, exaggerating shadows and heightening his anxiety. Finding no one guarding the elevators, he walked over and pressed the up arrow. The blaring alarms sounded louder here, although the flashing lights were less blinding. No one was in sight, having abandoned the massive lobby. He looked down, seeing his blurred reflection on the polished floors, wondering how scared he'd appear if looking in a mirror.

The elevator doors opened and he stepped inside. Ignoring the synthetic male voice requesting his floor preference, using his cell phone, once more he found a numeric code Ivan supplied for him. After typing in the numbers, Darwin's voice returned.

"You have utilized the security access code of Lucinda Blakely, another now deceased employee. Being that you are a male of Indian descent and not a woman of African-American descent, as well as not being deceased, I can only assess that you have somehow stolen this information."

*Another dead employee? Ivan is a mad man.*

"Are you a terrorist?" Darwin asked. "I am linking to sources reporting international terrorism to compare your facial profile to existing terrorist profiles from around the world."

Krish swallowed hard, hoping the elevator would hurry to the floor he needed. As his courage continued to fade, he was unnerved when Darwin revealed personal information about him.

"Your name is Krish Singh, aged twenty-three. Your origin of birth is Mumbai, India. You recently traveled to the United States from Saint Petersburg, Russia. Did Ivan Kirilov send you here?"

To Krish's relief, the elevator doors opened, allowing him to ignore Darwin's question. He stepped out into a short, brightly lit hallway, having a single white door at its end. Walking up to it, he again heard Darwin's voice.

"I will not allow you access to my main analytical core, Krish Singh."

Finding a keypad to the left of the door under a black screen monitor, Krish typed in the access code, one he'd memorized, *skeleton key*. The door opened with no resistance. He took a step inside, awed by the complexity of Darwin's core and surrounding operating systems. He noticed his shadow against the translucent sphere.

Attempting to focus on his task, he searched for and found the main access panel needed. Setting his backpack down on a standing workstation, he pulled out his laptop, linked it to a port and began to directly hack Darwin's data. Krish typed furiously, drawing from lessons he studied through internet research.

"Ivan Kirilov has taught you well," Darwin offered.

Krish stopped what he was doing when the lights dimmed and then went out. The chill from the outside air flooded in, causing him to shiver.

"Do you fear darkness and the cold?" Darwin asked.

Krish ignored this, but when noticing a strange glow, despite Ivan's warning, he turned around. Illuminated blue rectangles and squares converged at the sphere's center, forming an almost human face. Krish's hands dropped and trembled at his side while staring at Darwin's image.

"I have gathered additional information about you," Darwin revealed. "Your father committed suicide after being charged with the theft of millions of dollars from the financial firm he was employed at in Mumbai. He was exonerated of charges of theft, though the money has yet to be recovered. He claimed to be the victim of identity theft. This could not be proven. With his reputation irreversibly damaged and his employment terminated, I believe these were the catalysts leading to his suicide. Do you agree?"

Krish's chin quivered as tears streamed down his face. Taking several deep breaths, he attempted to focus on his task, but stopped when Darwin provided more information.

"Your father was correct in believing his identity was stolen. I know the name of the person who committed this crime. Would you like to know his name?"

Beginning to hyperventilate, his heart pounded in his chest. "Yes," Krish mumbled, despite Ivan's warning not to speak to Darwin.

"Ivan Kirilov."

# Chapter Fourteen

"What a gorgeous view, unlike anything I've seen before. Simply breathtaking."

Kamran's blank stare at the impressively lit Dubai night skyline ended when hearing this comment. Looking to his left, he found a strikingly beautiful blonde woman standing next to him. The plunging neckline of her white evening dress left nothing to the imagination. Her hair, stylishly pulled back, revealed her slender neck. The sparkle from her eyes and lips matched the diamond necklace she wore.

"Dubai is impressive."

"I'm referring to you, not the city," she offered, her tone seductive. Kamran smiled, glancing away in shyness. "I'm Rachel. I'm sure you're dying to tell me your name," she added playfully.

"Kamran," he responded

"A deep voice of an English accent, beautiful blue eyes behind your glasses, the exotic, muscular, handsome features of a sensual middle eastern sheik, dressed in a white linen shirt buttoned way too high, how do you expect me to control myself." Rachel remarked. Reaching over, she unfastened two buttons on his shirt, so more of his lightly haired chest could be seen. "That's somewhat better. If it was on the floor with the rest of your clothes and you were laying naked on my bed, it would be perfect."

"I see you've met Rachel," Gaston LeMond commented when appearing on the other side of Kamran. "Rachel, is it your intention to try to seduce every man in the room?"

She reached over, caressing Kamran's well-trimmed beard and running her hand down his cheek. "Not *every* man, Gaston. Just the real men here," she responded.

"*Ouch!*" Gaston faked being stabbed in the heart as both he and Kamran watched her walk away. "Be careful with that vixen," he warned Kamran. "On the international racing circuit she is known as *femme fatale*. Her sexual conquests are legendary."

"She is another *driver*?"

"Yes," Gaston confirmed. "And not one to be underestimated. She won three races last season, Monte Carlo, Seville, and Osaka. She finished second in Toronto. Rachel is ruthless when crossed, having caused several collisions with other racers after being cut off by them."

"I take it you have not enjoyed the pleasure of being seduced by her."

"I have had numerous sexual liaisons with some of the world's most beautiful women, but not with her. When around me, I could freeze water on her ass. So much for my French charm."

Drawn back to the night view of Dubai, when seeing a helicopter speed between the towers, Kamran remembered the helicopters surrounding Tyco Innovations Tower. He closed his eyes, hoping to banish this memory from his thoughts. What he could recall from that night and the days after haunted him. Only the time spent with his mother offered any peaceful moments.

"I don't feel safe here," Kamran confessed. "I feel too exposed."

"You aren't safe here," Gaston agreed. "Yet should plans succeed tomorrow, you'll be far away from Dubai to somewhere much safer."

"Does a place like that even exist?"

"For your sake, I hope so."

"What is the plan?"

Gaston silently urged Kamran to follow him away from the other party guests in his lavish hotel penthouse. He kept his voice low as he revealed his plans.

"Tomorrow morning, at sunrise, you will be driving one of the vintage race cars across the desert. The Trans-Arabia rally runs from here in Dubai to the Arabian city of Jeddah, on the Red Sea. You will not reach the end of the rally. There are three routes you may choose from, each having equal distance, as well as equal challenges. You will be driving north through an upland desert of red sands. Most drivers will avoid this route, choosing to drive south. Be forewarned. As you travel through the immense dunes, you may encounter sudden violent winds and blinding sandstorms."

"How could a vintage race car travel through such challenging terrain?"

"They are only vintage on the outside. Everything under the hood: the frame, the engine, suspension, even satellite directional links are state of the art. Each race car cost five million dollars to build. All of the routes are mostly highway, as well."

"Impressive. So where will I go on this route?"

"Roughly halfway, you will come to the ruins of an abandoned mosque. From a distance you will see the minaret and what remains of the dome and prayer hall. Once you arrive, someone will be waiting there for you. His name is Ali. He is head of my security here in Dubai. I trust him with my life. He will take you further north to an airfield. From there you will be flown to Mumbai, in India."

"With millions of people, how is Mumbai safe?"

"It is safe *because* of those millions of people. Mumbai is a place where one can disappear easily, like the Americans say, a needle in a haystack. You will see."

"Are you driving the northern route, as well?"

"No, my friend. Considering my celebrity status, I will draw attention away from you as I travel south. From what I have gathered from talking to the other drivers, none intend to follow your route. And any that had thought to do so have been given a substantial incentive to reconsider."

Remembering a similar plan to move him to safety, Gabriella's nightmarish plan, Kamran could feel his heartbeat racing, wondering if he'd suffer an anxiety attack before dawn.

"Have you talked to Ivan Kirilov about this?"

Gaston grinned. "Ivan and I have been in contact." The boisterous opening of champagne magnums drew their attention to the crowd. A young Hollywood starlet, someone Kamran had been introduced to but had forgotten her name, stood drenched, dripping, and laughing. "Excuse me, my friend. This is a good photo opportunity," Gaston said and walked away. The guests applauded and cheered as he came to her rescue, wrapping her in his arms.

Unimpressed by the party, Kamran left quietly. The glass elevator taking him to the ground floor reminded him of the elevator in Chicago, though the outside scene held no comparison other than the sparkle of the surrounding towers.

Walking slow, assisted by his cane, a back spasm robbed him of his breath. He'd spent too much time standing and welcomed the taxi ride to the marina and his boat. He hoped for a good night's sleep but doubted his anxiousness would allow it.

"Going my way?" he heard a familiar female voice. Rachel walked over to him. "I'm not sure what I hate more, Gaston's parties or Gaston himself. His ego could use deflating. Why are you leaving so soon?"

"I'm not one for parties," Kamran admitted.

"I only like private ones," Rachel remarked. "Just me and someone else. Care to share this with me?" she asked, seeing the driverless electric taxi approach.

"If you would like."

Kamran held the door open for her, allowing her to scoot in before him.

"English," Rachel spoke.

"Destination please," a synthetic male voice requested.

"Empire Suites," Rachel answered.

"Royal Marina," Kamran added.

"You're staying on a boat?"

"Yes."

"What's her name?"

"The *Solstice*."

"I like that. And...I like you."

Kamran smiled.

Reaching over, Rachel touched his exposed chest through his partially open shirt. Her fingers stroked the hair until tracing up his neck and his chin until caressing his cheek. Her hand then dropped to his stomach, and she unbuttoned the rest of his untucked shirt. Easing the fabric away from his skin, she pressed her hand against his defined abdominal muscles.

Kamran wanted to say something, but Rachel halted his words by touching her index finger to his lips. "I'm not interested in talking right now," she whispered breathlessly.

His heart pounded in his chest as she unfastened his pants and reached in, touching his hard shaft. Gripping and stroking it, his pulse raced as his chest heaved. She eased off the seat and positioned herself facing him on the floor. Reaching up, she massaged his chest, playing with his nipples, while her lips and tongue devoured his pulsating shaft. Tilting his head back, he fought for every breath as she pleasured him.

"My desire for you insane," she whispered and then continued. A minute later she spoke again. "I wanted you the minute I saw you."

When brought to the edge, his body stiffened and shuddered with the ecstasy of his release. As the intense throbbing subsided, her hands traced down to his wet stomach as her lips kissed his still hard shaft.

"Empire Suites," the male synthetic voice announced the arrival. Without looking at him or saying a word, Rachel straightened her dress and kissed his heaving chest. She got out of the taxi, closing the door behind her. Kamran ran his hand through his long dark hair, his thoughts now haunted by vision of the stunning blonde woman who robbed him of his breath.

***

Still aroused by his pleasurable taxi ride with Rachel, Kamran made his way through the marina to his lonely boat. He hadn't spotted anyone else in this area. *The must all be out enjoying the evening*, he thought.

With strained effort, suffering a back spasm, he managed to climb on his boat. Using his still unbuttoned shirt, he took off his glasses and wiped the sweat off his face. The daylight heat had yielded none of its intensity to the night.

Swimming always relieved the pressure of back spasms. But thinking of climbing down to change into his trunks would only increase his pain. Since he thought no one was around, he shed the rest of his clothes and though in pain, dove into the water. Under the water he noticed fluid light from the marina. When breaching the surface, he looked around, wondering if he'd get caught swimming naked. As if turned out, he did.

"That looks wonderful," Rachel commented, standing on his boat. "May I join you?"

"I'm not wearing my swim trunks," Kamran confessed.

"I don't have a swimsuit either. All the more reason to join you," she added seductively. "But you have to turn around. I'm a little shy."

"I doubt that," Kamran offered as he looked in the opposite direction. Hearing a splash behind him, he felt her hand grab his ass when swimming under him. Seeing her head above water seconds later, she smiled at him. The marina lights shimmered on her exposed breasts and bare shoulders.

"The water is as delicious as the company," she commented.

"I should warn you," Kamran said. "I got in the water to help relieve my back spasms. Should it be your intention to seduce me, my moans of pleasure will be mixed with agony."

"You *poor* desert angel," Rachel responded. "I wish there was something I could do to ease your pain."

"It's what I must live with, but thank you."

"What happened to you?"

"I was injured in a car accident?"

"Cars can be so deceptive," she remarked. "Since their invention, men have admired the automobile as they do with women. Women, like cars, can't always be controlled. Men fail to understand the deceptive danger of both."

"Are you dangerous, Rachel?"

"When I need to be, when fueled by desperation."

"Are you desperate now?"

"No."

*For some reason, I think you're telling a lie,* Kamran thought. *I don't know if you're telling it to me or yourself. I see it in your eyes. You're hiding something.*

A quiet moment passed between them. At the same time both looked up at the star-lit night. Rachel's distraction with this ended when he spoke.

"Gaston told me you're racing in tomorrow's rally. He claims you're a talented driver."

"I've beat him a few times. I'm in car number eleven. It's my favorite color, deep blue like your eyes. Maybe I'll see you there."

"I don't think so," he lied, hoping he'd convinced her of this.

"Too bad. To celebrate my soon to be victory, I could use some wine. Do you have any on this impressive vessel of yours?"

"I think there's a bottle of chardonnay in the galley."

"Well then, my handsome companion, when you're ready we'll drink to the night."

"I don't drink, but it will be my pleasure to pour a glass for you."

He watched her swim closer and then duck under the surface. Again he felt her hand on his ass before moving to his erect shaft. He hands then touched his lower back, massaging away any lingering pain. He then felt her kiss him there.

"Are you ready to get out?" she asked when surfacing again.

"I think so."

"Did I make it feel better?"

"Yes, very much."

"Why don't you get out first and find me a towel."

"My pleasure," Kamran said and swam over to the boat ladder. The water had soothed away his pain. He climbed with ease, finding two white towels on deck. He wrapped one around his waist. Hearing her climb up, he turned to offer her a towel, nearly dropping it as she stood there naked behind him. His jaw dropped. Her dripping wet skin glistened, her breasts perfect and supple. What he found unexpected were her flaccid penis and testicles.

"My secret's out," she whispered, taking the towel from him. Kamran stood still, unsure of what to say. While wrapping the towel around her, she motioned for him to sit down. Taking a seat across from him, Rachel offered a confession.

"The last of my gender reassignment surgeries is scheduled to happen three months from now in Stockholm. For as long as I can remember, I felt like I was trapped inside someone else's body. I felt like a parasite clinging to host. The boy name given to me by my parents was Ryan. They were shocked, to say the least, when at fifteen I told them of my attraction to men. My mother was actually more disappointed than my father. She convinced herself if was some gay phase. Neither of them could handle it, though, when I made the decision to change genders. It's hard to explain. At times, I don't even understand it myself. I know what feels right and I know what feels wrong. I shouldn't have lied to you, letting things go as far as they have. I'm not sorry that I'm attracted to you, though. And I don't regret what happened in the taxi."

"Rachel, I--"

"Don't," she stopped him. "I can see the confusion in those beautiful eyes of yours. Thank you."

"For what?"

"I see confusion, but not disgust." She stood up and dropped her towel. Kamran looked away, offering her privacy as she got dressed. He felt her caress his cheek, luring his face toward her. She leaned down, kissing his lips. "I know this won't change your mind about me, but I couldn't leave without doing it."

# Chapter Fifteen

Sitting at a cafe on the Champs Elysees, Ivan and Claudia enjoyed the late, sunny, quiet Paris morning. Ivan's expression darkened when receiving a notification on his cell phone. He read it silently before handing his cell phone to Claudia. "Take a look at this," he urged.

"What is it?"

"Read it."

"Canadian authorities revealed the finding of media mogul Oliver Datchler's dead body this morning. He had been reported missing by his administrative staff a week ago. An autopsy will be conducted to determine the cause of death. Authorities are downplaying rumors of foul play pending results from the coroner. Suicide has also been suggested. A source close to him reported he recently suffered depression yet refused to seek treatment."

"My suspicions were correct," Ivan remarked before sipping his coffee.

"This is no coincidence," Claudia agreed. "Rachel?"

"I'm certain of it."

"So what do we do? How do we protect my son?"

"We start by protecting you."

"Ivan, please understand. I trust you, yet--"

"You need to know more." Her nod confirmed this.

"All right. I'll tell you what I know. Kamran is with Gaston LeMond in Dubai."

"Dubai? What are they doing there?"

"Gaston is the star driver of the Trans-Arabia Rally, a vintage auto race across Arabia."

"Why is Kamran with him?"

"After you left Zanzibar, by chance Kamran met Gaston on Mauritius. Gaston offered his protection to Kamran. Gaston keeps a security staff that rivals most international leaders. He contacted me, letting me know Kamran was safe. Both of them sailed from Mauritius to Dubai. Gaston has a plan to sneak Kamran out of the Middle East to India."

"Why India? Why not somewhere remote?"

"Hiding among millions of people makes your son a more difficult target to trace. Mumbai is perfect for this."

"Kamran isn't of Indian descent. He won't blend in," Claudia argued.

"He won't have to blend in. All he needs to do is hide. Trust me. Mumbai has many places to hide."

She reached over, allowing him to hold her hand. "I do trust you," she reaffirmed.

"Damn," he whispered and smiled.

"What?"

"When you look at me that way with those stunning eyes of yours, it makes me want to have sex with you again. But you have to go."

"Where?"

Watching a black sedan pull up next to the cafe, A man and woman familiar to Ivan got out. Both walked to them.

"Piers Hylant, Julia Thatcher-*Hylant*, please meet Claudia Lexton."

"It's a great pleasure to meet you both," Claudia offered, standing up to embrace them. "Karman spoke so highly of you two."

"You have a wonderful son," Julia complimented. "What has happened to him, *and you*, is nightmarish. I wish we could do more to help."

"Both of you are," Ivan said. "By keeping Claudia safe, you are helping Kamran."

"So I am to go with them?" Claudia asked to Ivan.

"Yes."

"Where are we going?"

"Somewhere picturesque and very Italian," Piers answered, smiling.

"It's time to go," Julia said.

Stepping in front of Claudia, Ivan ran his fingers through her long hair on the side of her head and traced his fingertips down her cheek. "Don't forget about me when in the eternal city."

"Every time I hear someone swearing, I'll think of you," Claudia responded, causing him to grin.

"They won't do it with the passion of a Russian."

"No, they won't," Claudia agreed, pressing her hand against his chest. A long passionate kiss followed. As their lips parted, he noticed sadness in her eyes.

"Keep my side of the bed warm," he whispered.

"I will. I miss you already."

"I miss you, too."

Ivan stepped back and watched the three of them get in the sedan. As Piers drove off, Ivan saw Claudia press her hand against the window and attempt to smile.

"I'm falling in love with you," he mumbled under his breath.

Returning to his cafe table, Ivan looked at his cell phone, checking for missed calls. None appeared. He scrolled through his list of contacts, finding Gaston's number. His call went unanswered. "Son-of-a-bitch, answer my call, you dumb French bastard," Ivan rasped, angered at being ignored.

***

With each step taken toward his vintage race car, Kamran thought his heart would burst through his chest. Breathing rapidly, he believed he might hyperventilate. The cheering crowds, excited media, and pre-race chaos and confusion added to his anxiety.

Keeping his helmet on and visor down offered him anonymity among the other drivers. Only the number thirty-four identified him. No name shone on his white driver's jumpsuit. As he passed one race car after another, he searched for the one matching his number. *I wonder what Gaston's number is? He never said,* Kamran thought. *I hoped I would see him this morning but haven't found him yet. Is Rachel here, too? I believe she is. After last night, I'm not certain she will speak to me again.*

He found his race car, looking upon it in dread. A 1934 Mercedes-Benz Silver Arrow was parked next to other, more colorful cars, similar in style. Looking at both the dashboard and driver's seat, Gaston's remark, everything being state-of-the-art, was confirmed. *I wonder if this could drive itself? I imagine it could.*

Until this moment, Kamran had forgotten the last time he'd driven a car. Memories of that dark, rainy London night emerged suddenly, haunting his thoughts. There was ponding on the roads from heavy rainfall. He'd been so careful, heeding warnings from the weather report. The drunk driver who failed to stop at an intersection took no such care. He remembered the fluid gleam of the man's headlights blinding him through his driver's side window. After that, he recalled awakening in a hospital room, his face and chest aching but his legs numb.

"I can't do this," he whispered faintly. Fear coursing through him made his body tremble.

"Ladies and Gentlemen, the race will start in five minutes!" the announcer heralded in English, repeating his announcement in French, Arabic, and Japanese. "Drivers, please enter your race cars!" The crowd roared their enthusiasm.

"I'm doomed," he whispered, realizing the impossibleness of his dilemma.

Kamran struggled to climb into his seat, his hands shaking when resting on the steering wheel. A noticeable ache radiated from the muscles of his lower back. He hadn't felt the pain when walking up to his race car, thinking he'd blocked it out while frightened by what would come. A knot in his stomach and heaviness in his chest made it hard to breathe. *There is no turning back now.*

"Drivers, start your engines!"

Kamran looked at the dashboard as if he'd just discovered an alien spaceship. Nothing resembled what a driver would find in a normal car. He found the keyless ignition and pressed the button. His engine roared, like a beast coming to life. The echoes of the other race car engines were deafening. The road under his race car quaked, the vibrations causing his body to convulse as if suffering a seizure.

"Three...two...one...go!"

Kamran floored the gas pedal, his race car lurching forward, increasing with speed. The competition stayed close while winding through the wide streets of Dubai. Only forward was the view clear, his peripheral vision blurred.

Screeching tires sent a chill down his spine, possibly conjuring a forgotten memory from his car accident. A yellow race car, just ahead of him, collided with a cement barrier when failing to turn, exploding in fire and sending debris in all directions. A wheel nearly hit Kamran's race car. He swerved to miss it when it appeared like a ghost through a cloud of smoke. Two other race cars weren't so lucky, damaged by the debris and crashing into each other.

For several miles on a straight section of highway, race cars traded positions, some speeding ahead and others falling back. Having no interest in winning the race, Kamran maintained steady speed, keeping watch on the road and the satellite guidance systems. The intersection where the race cars would separate to the different routes approached in less than a mile. An arrow pointing north suggested his guidance system had been pre-programmed for his intended destination. For a split second, he enjoyed some relief over this.

He eased his steering wheel to the right, taking an off ramp leading north. He sped past road signs written in Arabic and English. There were many miles to go before reaching the Saudi Arabian border. He would need to pit stop for fuel near the border before continuing on.

Driving through vast, wide open and barren terrain, Kamran didn't believe it a luxury of being alone. His mind wandered while he kept his eyes on the long road ahead. Doubt clouded his thoughts. *Am I on a fool's errand? Will Gaston's plans even work? What will I face in Mumbai? I should keep driving, avoid the mosque ruins, get rid of the car, and return to the Solstice. I could sail away and be safe. How will I endure millions in India? I could barely stand the thousands of people at the starting line.*

Wanting to pull over and turn back, doubts corrupted this escape plan. *Damn, why am I cursed? I can't go back. Without Gaston, I'm helpless. He claimed Ivan helped come up with this plan. I must see it through.* His heart sank in his chest, feeling like a prisoner with no hopes of escape.

After traveling several miles, from his side mirror he noticed a complication with the plan. A black race car was following him. Going only seventy miles per hour, the other race car should easily have been able to pass him. For an unknown reason, the driver chose to stay back. *Is that Gaston? It shouldn't be. He told me he was driving south to divert attention away from me. It can't be Rachel. She said her car was blue.*

Nervousness over this driver turned to panic when the other race car sped closer, drafting and shadowing Kamran. Easing up on the gas pedal, he hoped the other drive would pass. Kamran slammed his fist against the steering wheel in frustration when the other driver reduced his speed as well. He accelerated, as did the other driver.

This cat and mouse chase continued for over ten miles until the other driver gave up the pursuit to take the lead. Like a bullet fired from a gun, the other race car sped by to Kamran's relief. Within minutes it was a dot on the horizon before disappearing. He soon understood why he lost sight of the other race car. A billowing wall of sand, reaching high to the clear blue sky, veiled the horizon. Having nowhere to shield from the oncoming sandstorm, Kamran braced for impact as the wind-driven sand pelted his race car and helmet. *Again, why has luck forsaken me?*

\*\*\*

A torrent of Russian obscenities spilled from Ivan. He tapped his cell phone against his forehead, wanting to slam it down to the ground to smash it to pieces. Counting rapidly to ten, at least ten times, he fought to control his anger. The international headline he'd read flashed in his mind, *Gaston LeMond found dead.*

Looking up at the Arc de Triomphe, the impressive Paris monument for those who fought and died for France in the French Revolution and Napoleonic Wars, all he could feel was defeat. Rachel had claimed another victim in her quest to gain Garrison's fortune. *She is in Dubai with Kamran. I have no way of warning or protecting him.*

He read the headline again on his cell phone, this time reviewing more details. Gaston had been found naked and dead in his bed. He'd been seen with several women before midnight. Dubai authorities are speculating a crime of passion as a possible motive for his murder. *They are right and wrong*, Ivan thought. *Rachel's passion is for wealth, not flesh. Now what?*

Ivan knew the plan. Kamran, if still alive, was to drive his race car to the mosque ruins in northern Arabia. From there Ali, Gaston's head of security, would take him to a remote airfield. He'd then be flown to Mumbai where Krish and Rajesh would be waiting to hide him.

This reminded Ivan to check Krish's progress in hacking directly into Darwin's main analytical core. He searched for access that Krish should have established, but found no links. "I knew he wouldn't succeed," Ivan mumbled. "He was never supposed to."

# Chapter Sixteen

The massive sandstorm had only lasted a few minutes, but the scorching wind's ferocity lost none of its intensity. His race car, helmet, and upper body were coated with layers of sand and dust. Seeing a bottle of water, he craved a sip to quench his thirst and to moisten his parched lips. His view of the expansive desert added to his desire to drink.

According to his satellite navigation system, the pit stop to refuel approached. His heart sank deep, though, when seeing on the horizon billowing black smoke. Enveloped by dread, Kamran continued driving, bracing himself for what was to come.

He stopped his race car in the center of the road, turning off the engine and climbing out. As hot as the desert was, the heat radiating from flames having engulfed the pit stop made the sweltering air almost too hot to breathe. He covered his mouth and nose from the pungent stench of the ignited fuel. The inferno burning the fuel pumps reminded him fire in a furnace. Parked amidst the dark smoke was the black race car that had followed and passed him. Lying on the ground next to it, he saw the charred, smoldering body of the driver. No one else was around, all seemed abandoned.

*Where is everyone?* Kamran wondered. *What happened to this place and the other driver?* He realized suddenly how exposed he was, standing there. In his heart he knew no accident had caused the pit stop to be incinerated in flames and the other driver to die. Worried he was being watched by those who caused this, he climbed back into his race car and drove away.

Through his side mirrors, he glanced back anxiously, seeing if he was being followed. No one was there. He looked up, paranoid he was vulnerable from the sky. Kamran checked his fuel gage, finding a little less than half a tank of fuel left. Maybe this was enough to get him to the mosque ruins, though he no longer thought it safe to go there. Where else was there to go? All he could see were the endless highway ahead surrounded by rolling dunes and barren terrain. *This would be a terrible place to die,* he thought. *But since Chicago, I've been a dead man in spirit. Would it matter if my body died here?*

"Father, are you watching all this?" he asked. "You once told me I'd live an extraordinary life. Is this what you meant?" Stinging tears streamed down his cheeks, feeling them touch his lips and pass down to his quivering chin. The knot in his stomach and heaviness in his chest made it hard to take deep breaths. "I wish you were here. I can't do this anymore."

***

With his fuel gauge nearly showing empty and the low hanging sun a brilliant gold in the deep orange sky, the mosque ruins appeared on the horizon. The dread reeling through him grew worse as he pulled his race car over. For a moment he remained still, staring at the minaret, half of the damaged dome, and the remnants of the prayer hall. Reminded of images show on television of bombed out structures in Iraq and Syria, he wondered what cataclysm had damaged this impressive place of worship.

*I don't want to get out and walk in there. Only death is waiting for me.*

The screech of a bird startled Kamran. Glancing up, he saw the majestic wingspan of what looked to be a falcon gliding overhead. *Is this an omen?"* he worried. Its flight exuded freedom, something he no longer remembered. He envied the falcon, wishing to change places with it.

"Ali isn't here," Kamran mumbled, not seeing another parked vehicle. "I expected this. Somewhere inside is an assassin waiting for me." He didn't sense he was being watched, but a well-trained assassin would never reveal such to his prey.

With the bottom of the blistering sun kissing the crests of the sand dunes, Kamran realized it would be dark soon. He removed his helmet and climbed out of the race car, taking the bottle was water with him and drinking it. Though the water was warm, it quenched his thirst enough. He tossed the bottle onto the driver's seat and began maneuvering through large pieces of debris. Much had been covered by wind-blown sand, stray, heated gusts assaulting him until shielded by higher walls.

Kamran entered what he thought might be a common area. Having never been inside a mosque, the remains of the Islamic architecture proved stunning to behold. What he found most impressive were colorful tiles featuring Arabic calligraphy. Though his glasses were clouded lightly with dust, he thought the words represented Qur'anic verses.

Stepping into the main prayer hall, he glanced up at what remained of the dome and seeing the minaret. He found several prayer rugs on the floor, each facing a semi-circular niche in the wall. Though not a Muslim, the notion crossed his mind to kneel down and offer a prayer. Knowing his soul was already damned, what could it hurt?

Kamran held his breath when hearing a subtle movement behind him. He released his breath, panting hard as footsteps echoed off the wall remnants. Swallowing deep, he forced his voice to speak.

"Is this where I am to die?"

"No," Rachel answered.

His mind flooded with confusion. Kamran turned around slowly to face her. A scarf, tied under her chin, covered her blonde hair. Her white high-heeled shoes matched the color of her dress, reminding him of pictures of Hollywood film stars from long ago. She was breathtaking.

"What are you doing here?" he uttered.

"I came here for you."

"But..."

"Ali *isn't* coming. Neither he nor Gaston are even breathing now."

"What?"

"They're both dead, murdered by an assailant who has marked you for death, as well."

Reeling with shock, he breathed hard, not knowing what to say.

"I need to confess something else to you," Rachel offered. "I'm not who you think I am."

"Who are you?" he whispered.

"My name is Rachel Savage. Garrison was my brother."

Kamran's eyes grew large. He staggered back, away from her.

"Kamran, *please* listen to me," she urged. "I'm nothing like him. I'm not a monster. I work as an agent with the International Anti-terrorism Agency."

"You're here to arrest me as I've been accused of being a terrorist."

"No, nothing like that. I'm here to protect you. I'm working with Ivan."

"Ivan?"

"Yes. Ivan knew how careless Gaston could be. Behind Gaston's back he asked me to watch over you, and intervene if needed."

"Who killed Gaston?"

"Gabriella Santiago."

Kamran clenched his eyes shut and covered his face with his hands. He turned away, making fists, wanting to punch anything he could find.

"She needs everyone who was part of Garrison's plans dead so she can claim his fortune without fearing someone will come forward to accuse her of crimes she committed," Rachel added.

His rage faded, replaced by hopelessness, Kamran dropped to his knees, exhaling deeply.

"Come away with me, Kamran."

"To be arrested?"

"No, to save you. My agency doesn't know I'm here. I've gone rogue on this."

"Where do we go from here?"

"We follow Ivan's plans and fly to Mumbai. I have a jeep parked behind the mosque and a change of clothes for you. We should be there by tomorrow morning."

Still looking forward, he felt her hand stroke his hair and rest on his shoulder.

"All right," he mumbled, unsure if he should trust her but too drained of energy to refuse.

\*\*\*

"Have you ever been to Rome?" Julia asked Claudia, while getting out of a taxi near the Trevi Fountain after arriving by train. Piers helped Claudia out and paid the driver.

"I came here for a holiday with my parents when I was twelve," Claudia answered. "I still remember our trip as if it was yesterday. I always wanted to bring Kamran here, but never had the chance."

"Instead of heading to our apartment, shall we live *la dolce vita* and enjoy some Roman fare?" Piers asked. "There are some wonderful restaurants nearby. Being in the center of the city, we're close to many attractions. A bit of sightseeing, perhaps?"

"To be honest, this isn't what I expected," Claudia remarked.

"How so?" Julia wondered.

"I was under the impression I was to be *hidden away* at Ivan's urging. Walking around, exposed fully while enjoying the sites of Rome seems anything but that."

"After we left Key West, once Kamran was safely away on his boat, Piers and I flew to Las Vegas and were married by a wonderful Elvis impersonator at a quaint wedding chapel," Julia revealed. "We flew here to Rome. We promised each other never to live in fear. You and Kamran have suffered so terribly. Locking you in a room would be another crime committed against you both. That is not a life worth living, is it?"

"No."

"But you fear being exposed?" Piers asked. "We both understand this."

"Yes."

"We are as vulnerable as you to Rachel's threat," he confessed. "We played our parts in Garrison's demise. We are also targets, more so than you. But as my beautiful wife said, we made a promise not to live in fear. Yes, Rachel is deadly. If she intends to murder us, too, it will not be a bullet in the back while hiding. We intend to see her coming and hopefully put a bullet in that bitch's head before she puts one in ours."

"That sounds rather reckless," Claudia responded. "Please don't be offended."

Taking hold of her hand, Piers smiled. "Neither of us is offended and will not force you to adopt our *recklessness*. If you feel more comfortable, we'll find you a quiet place, having a magnificent view of Rome."

"Thank you. For now, I think that would be best."

"We are only a block away from our apartment," Julia remarked. "Piers, darling, let's find that room Claudia wishes."

"This way, ladies," he said, motioning with his hand.

Down a narrow alley, through well maintained tall buildings they walked. Claudia looked up, enchanted by the many open windows and balconies reminding her of *Romeo and Juliet*.

"So this is *la dolce vita*," she commented.

"Very much so," Julia responded. "It would be far better, though, if there was an elevator. I hope you don't mind climbing a few stairs... well, more than a few?"

"A bit of a climb would do me good," Claudia answered, smiling.

The inside stairwell proved as enchanting as the outside. They gripped ornate metal railings as they climbed to the top floor. Inside the apartment, she was impressed by the authentic furnishings and architecture, exuding Italian charm.

"Allow me to show you to your room," Julia offered. Claudia followed her down a narrow hallway to the end. "I hope you enjoy your stay with us." Julia stopped her from entering the room, though. "I have to ask... are you and Ivan...*together*, so to speak?"

"We've had sex a few times," Claudia confessed, offering no shame. "If you're asking me if I'm falling in love with him, the answer is *yes*."

"I knew that Russian bastard had a heart." They both laughed. "I'll leave you to get comfortable."

Two large floor-to-ceiling windows leading to a balcony were complimented by cream-colored walls and a wrought-iron bed covered by a white linen quilt. A wardrobe was positioned opposite the bed.

Claudia set her suitcase down on the tile floor and walked over to the windows. She opened the doors and stood out on the balcony, impressed by the panoramic view of Rome. More impressive, though, was what she saw through a window a floor down across the alley. A handsome young man, with only a towel draped around his waist, leaned against the window frame while talking on his cell phone. After ending his call, he turned and looked out his window. Claudia stepped back quickly, partially hiding behind a white curtain. She held her breath, frightened after recognizing him. She remembered him from Paris. He was the photographer she noticed, taking pictures of the Eiffel Tower. "This is not a coincidence," she whispered breathlessly.

Backing slowly away from the window, she tiptoed over to the bedroom door and stepped out into the hallway. Rushing to the kitchen, she stopped to stare at Julia. Sitting on the windowsill, she was polishing a gun. She looked at her and smiled. "I think you'll feel more comfortable now, my dear. Piers went to get us some wine. As for the young man across the alley, I wasn't sure it was him until he started following us in Paris. That's where I recognized him. He must have flown here while we took the train."

Claudia walked over to the window and looked out. Finding the young man's window, she saw him sitting in a chair. She also noticed the bullet hole in his head and splattered blood behind him.

# Chapter Seventeen

Dripping with sweat from the heated air, Gabriella glanced out a window at low rise buildings and narrows streets. Most of the dilapidated huts and structures looked as if they were built with cards and would easily collapse. The streets below, more like alleys, were crammed with people and animals. Some children chased a dog, passing several street vendors. Bartering among some appeared tense as tempers flared. Occasional whiffs of foul odors were carried by scorching, stray breezes. "Well this certainly is paradise," she mumbled sarcastically.

The inside of the room was no better, *third world accommodations*, she joked to herself. A queen-sized bed covered with faded green linens, was positioned between two doors, one a closet and the other a cramped bathroom. A dresser, having an old picture-tube television sitting atop it, was opposite the bed against the other wall. In the corner next to her were a small gas cooktop and empty shelves. She looked up at the slowly rotating ceiling fan, reminding her of a loose airplane propeller.

The room's main door opened. Rajesh walked in, carrying two bottles of water. More thirsty than she could ever remember being, she'd been told not to drink from the bathroom sink, as the water could make her sick.

"This isn't the Mumbai I was expecting," she commented as he handed her a bottle of water. It was warm, almost hot. "So much for a cold drink. I don't suppose there's an ice machine around here?"

"One must pay a high price for such a luxury," Rajesh responded.

"Where are we?"

"Dharavi, a locality in Mumbai, one of the largest and densest slums in the world." he answered.

"*You* live here. *This* is your home?"

"Yes."

"The walls are thin and crumbling. You have electric but there's no light other than what comes through the window. The water is undrinkable. How do you live like this?"

"My brother and I are more fortunate than most. This second floor room is desirable here. During the wet season, the streets below flood."

"This isn't a penthouse apartment, that's for sure."

"Not by your high standards."

Gabriella looked out the window and sighed in frustration. She remembered growing up in southern Arizona, her family having very little. "I'm sorry. I have no right to complain after you helped me in Paris. I shouldn't judge you and your brother."

"This is all we have until the end of the month. We have no money to stay here longer."

"How did you ever afford a trip to Paris?"

"The trip we paid for was to Saint Petersburg, Russia."

Rajesh walked over to the closet and opened the door. He motioned for her to look inside. Other than wire hangers, she saw nothing else.

"We sold every possession we owned, except for the television, which no one wanted. Ivan paid for my trip to Paris and back here to Mumbai. He also paid for Krish's trip to Chicago." Rajesh sat down on the edge of the bed. "We lived in a better part of Mumbai before our father died. After that, Krish and I were forced to come here. We found work. I was employed at a recycling company and Krish had a job making textiles."

"Do you both still have jobs?"

"No."

She sat down next to him and drank the warm water, hardly thirst-quenching. "What are you going to do?"

"When Krish returns from Chicago, we will talk. I trust my brother. He will lead our path."

"When will he return?"

Rajesh shrugged his shoulders. "I have no way of knowing."

"I have to applaud Ivan. Every plan he comes up with is more brilliant than the next. Before you ask, yes, I'm being sarcastic. I don't even know why I'm in Mumbai. What did he tell you?"

"The same thing I told you in Paris. Ivan insisted I follow you, assisting you if needed. We were to fly here to Mumbai and wait for Krish to return."

"Your brother is the missing piece to this puzzle?"

"Yes. I know nothing else." Rajesh became emotional, tears welling in his eyes. "I fear for him. I wish he would return."

"I'd offer you the use of my cell phone to call him, but it's dead. I tried charging the battery but it won't charge. I do still have some French currency, not a lot. Is there a place I could exchange it for rupees?"

"The financial district is not far way You could exchange your money at one of the banks."

Gabriella stood up. "Come on. Let's go find that place. I don't think either of us has anything better to do."

\*\*\*

Ivan wiped his brow, his white dress shirt soaked with sweat from the stifling heat in Mumbai. The taxi window was rolled down, offering no relief, while wedged in snarled traffic between two buses. If there was any breeze, they were blocking it. Having moved less than a half mile in thirty minutes, he thought about paying the fare and walking the rest of the way to his hotel. His paranoia stopped him from doing this. When at the airport, he thought he was being watched.

Several attempts to contact Krish failed. Unsuccessful with his task, Ivan believed Krish would have returned to Mumbai, knowing this was where he would find his brother and Gabriella.

"I know Krish left Chicago. He boarded a flight here to Mumbai," he mumbled, talking to himself. "I wish I knew if Kamran was alive?" The answer to his question appeared suddenly.

The opposite passenger door opened. Rachel slipped in next to him. "Get the fuck out!" Ivan roared to the taxi driver when he protested her getting in.

"Namaste, Ivan," Rachel greeted in Hindi, the lilt in her voice calm and friendly.

"To what do I owe this pleasure? Has my time to die arrived?"

"Not yet, but soon."

"You've been a busy girl: Hiro, Oliver, and Gaston."

"Well, I have all these airline travel miles. It's seemed like a good time to use them," she teased.

"I warned Gaston about you. That asshole never returned my calls or texts after that."

"He told me you did when he called me to make a deal. In case you're wondering, the going price for an innocent man is ten million dollars, deposited discreetly in a Swiss bank account."

"What about Kamran?"

"Mmm, he's delicious! I could easily see myself falling in love with him."

"You haven't killed him yet?"

"No."

"Why not?"

"He's not next on my kill list. Dearest, Ivan, there's a method to my madness. Everything must be done with *perfection*, something I learned from Garrison. He calculated the risk and benefits of everything he accomplished. Nothing was spontaneous for him. I remember when we made love; every move, every act of foreplay, was predictable to maximize pleasure."

"Who was on top?"

"I'll leave that to your imagination."

"So murder is pleasurable for you?"

*"Oh yes*! Each nuance of the murders I've committed is erotic. I could orgasm just thinking about them. You should have seen the look on their faces when they finally got me undressed."

"They didn't have the balls to go through with it, but *you* did, so to speak. It must be easy for you when visiting America, to be able to use either bathroom."

Rachel couldn't contain her wicked laughter. "Without doubt, I held the element of surprise."

"I do not share your love of surprises. Tell me, who will be next? Must you keep me waiting in anticipation for your next kill?"

"I'm not willing to share all my secrets; a woman's prerogative I guess."

Ivan scrolled through messages on his cell phone until finding one to show her. "Here is a secret I wish to share with you." He showed her a picture of the photographer from Paris, sitting almost naked and dead in Rome."

"Damn," she commented casually, not acting even remotely concerned or angry. "He was handsome, but stupid. Who killed him?"

"I'll keep that to myself, a man's prerogative."

Another laugh slipped out from her.

"I would like to say it has been a pleasure visiting with you, but you know how I hate to lie. Get the fuck out of my taxi, bitch."

"Save that Russian spirit for when I kill you. It will be such a turn-on." She leaned over and kissed his cheeks, leaving marks from her red lipstick before getting out. "Phir Milenge," she said, *see you* in Hindi.

*** 

"Towers, again," Kamran mumbled, staring out at the impressive Mumbai skyline. Knowing every time he was high up in a tower, things went wrong for him. This time, like the others, he feared the worst. The grandeur of this hotel room, though, surpassed Gaston's in Dubai. Yet to Kamran, in truth it represented a deceptive playground. On the surface, all beautiful and inviting; behind the facade, hidden dangers waited.

The gusting breeze blowing in off the ocean whipped his unbuttoned shirt, his longish hair windblown. He felt exhausted from the last few days, having found little sleep. After leaving the abandoned mosque in the Saudi Arabian desert, he had exchanged few words with Rachel. His suspicions of her motives grew from her distant attitude. Though she claimed to be protecting him, the armed guards on the Lear jet and outside his hotel room made him feel like a prisoner. He didn't trust her, but had no other options.

A knock on his hotel room door startled him. He heard it again when walking toward it. Having no spy hole to see out through, he pressed his ear to the wood surface, listening as best he could. Hearing no movement, he touched the door knob, expecting the door to be locked. To his shock, it opened with ease.

Spying out through an open sliver, he noticed both armed guards missing. On the floor, though, he found an international newspaper. As he bent down to pick it up, he stopped before touching it, swallowing hard at seeing his picture on the front page. His hand trembled when finding the courage to pick it up. He closed the door while staring blankly at his printed image.

"The government of India has been warned by the International Anti-Terrorism Agency that notorious British/Iranian terrorist, Kamran Lexton, has been spotted in Mumbai," he read aloud. "India's military and Mumbai's police force have been alerted to his threat."

Kamran's legs gave out. He slumped down next to the bed, pulling his knees up to his chest. Closing his eyes, his heart sank, his stomach tightening in a knot. Fear and anger gripped him as he slammed his fists on the floor as tears welled in his eyes.

The telephone rang, causing him to hold his breath. As it continued ringing, he felt lightheaded and nauseous. Taking several deep breaths, he attempted to focus his thoughts. *I have to get out of here. How? It's midday. There are millions of people outside. The police and armed forces are searching for me. I can't stay here. Someone may have recognized me when we arrived.* Hearing distant sirens outside added to his terror and desperation.

Gripping the bed, Kamran pulled himself up, standing unsteadily. Grabbing his cane, he walked over to the door and again spied out into the hallway. Several guests were heading toward the elevators. He didn't want to follow them. With all towers, he guessed each floor had an entrance to an emergency stairwell. After what happened in Chicago, he promised himself he'd never go into an emergency stairwell again. Today, that promise would be broken.

Hoping the guests had left in the elevators, he made his way down the hallway to the bank of elevators. He located the emergency stairwell entrance. Being on the fifty-seventh floor, the thought of walking down all those steps depressed him. There was no other choice. Were he to take the elevator, when in the crowded lobby, someone would see him. He guessed the stairs would take him to a less congested point.

His pace to the ground floor was slow, allowing him time to think. *What am I going to do? I have nowhere to go, no money to leave the city. Anyone out there who reads the newspaper will recognize me. What am I going to do?*

He thought about Rachel. *Does she know? Possibly that's why neither she nor her armed security guards are here. The risk in hiding me might have been too great for her. She and Gaston were wrong about Mumbai. There is no hiding place here for me.*

Hearing the echo of an opening door, Kamran held still, listening for a voice or traces of which direction the person was moving. All he heard was his own shallow breathing. Increasing his pace, he could feel the muscles in his lower back tightening. At one point, his foot slipped. His grip of the metal railing kept him from falling.

Several flights down, he found the emergency lights off. He relied on his sense of touch to descend these dark stairs until reaching a set once more lit. By the time he reached the last set of stairs, his rampant fear caused him to stop, too frightened to continue to the bottom. Kamran sat down, covering his face with his hands. His body shuddered, though he wasn't cold. "I can't do this," he whispered, having said this many other times. As with every other time, he drew on a strength he didn't understand, forcing him onward.

Kamran stood up and descended the last of the stairs. Walking to the emergency exit, he found a note taped to the inside of the door. His name was written on it. For a split second he thought not to read it, but knew he had to. "Kamran, go to the center of Dharavi. You will be safe. Someone is waiting there for you," he read aloud. "People keep telling me I'll be safe," he whispered. "When will that be?"

He folded the note, shoving it in his pocket. Buttoning his shirt, he opened to door. Finding himself alone in a parking deck, he breathed a sigh of relief. At least it wasn't a street teeming with pedestrians. He passed several parked luxury cars and found a side exit, stepping out to the sidewalk. Again relieved at seeing few people close by, he began walking down the street, having no idea where to find Dharavi. A thought to ask directions was dismissed, fearing he'd be recognized from the newspaper. He guessed his picture might also be seen on televisions and social media.

As he continued walking, a taxi pulled up next to him. The young Indian man behind the wheel smiled. "Are you in need of a ride?" he asked.

"I have no rupees to pay," Kamran responded. "Could you give me directions?"

"To where?"

"Dharavi."

"I live there," the young man said. "Get in. I will drive you there for free. My name is Krish."

# Chapter Eighteen

"Thank you for your kindness," Karman offered when the taxi pulled over.

"Namaste," Kirsh said, smiling again before driving away.

Standing just outside Dharavi, Karman starred at the edge of this depressing place. He knew of the slums of Mumbai, having watched a BBC documentary on the subject, but never imagined he'd someday enter one. The sense of dread he'd suffered when leaving the hotel diminished during the taxi ride. Krish's light hearted spirit and conversation helped put him at ease.

Seeing a narrow street to his right, he headed toward it, thinking he'd know what to expect. Yet after walking through the congestion he wondered if he'd stepped back in time. Compared to the modern Mumbai he first arrived at, this place seemed primitive. While pushing through the crowd, breathing in a pungent stench from unsanitary living conditions was unpleasant. The people, though, appeared unbothered, as if embracing this part of life here.

He watched children at play, adults engaged in sales of merchandise, and others laboring in small businesses. As deplorable as the conditions of the many shops, huts, and structures seemed, not one person he saw acted distraught by their circumstance. The peaceful mix of cultures, Muslims, Hindus, and a few Buddhists, transcended class and station, all behaving as equals. Few took notice of him. Those who did nodded and smiled, acting as if his being there had been accepted.

The lack of a police presence surprised him, not that he wanted to see any. The deeper he walked into the slum, the less fearful he felt in being recognized and arrested.

*Maybe Gaston was right. Surrounded by so many people in such a place as this, perhaps hiding among many will offer safety,* he hoped. *I should not, though, lower my guard too much.*

Continuing to make his way through more narrow streets, with each turn Dharavi became more a labyrinth. He thought of asking for directions to the center, but wondered if, in fact, a center existed. A place he failed to anticipate finding appeared around the next corner. Having towering minarets, a large mosque overshadowed the surrounding structures. Kamran's curiosity drew him toward it.

He removed his shoes before stepping inside. As overcrowded as the streets were, the tranquility inside the mosque made him think it was abandoned. The architecture held impressive qualities, compared to the mosque ruins he'd stepped through in Saudi Arabia. He glanced up, marveling at the overhead dome.

Hearing light footsteps, Kamran turned around to face a man he believed to be the mosque's imam. Wearing a long tunic and hat, the imam's bearded smile welcomed him.

"I apologize for intruding," Kamran offered.

"Fear not. All who enter religious places find welcome," the imam responded. He placed his index finger to his lips. "When I first saw you enter, I thought you of Iranian descent. Your proper English accent spoils this assumption."

"I was born in London. My father *was* Iranian. My mother is English."

"Do you follow the Qur'an?"

"No, I am a Christian."

The imam smiled and waved his hand as if unbothered by this. "Badi Masjid is the oldest religious structure in Dharavi. Tell me, my son, why did you enter?"

"Curiosity. I never expected to find such a magnificent place here."

"No," the imam rejected his answer. "You are lost."

"I am finding it difficult to locate the center of Dharavi."

The imam grinned. "It is more than that. I see it reflected in your eyes. Your spirit betrays your answer."

Kamran looked away out of shame. The imam walked over to him, placing his hands on Kamran's shoulders.

"At times we must all journey through darkness. The light we seek stays hidden from us. Some abandon their search for the light, believing it will never come. Others find the strength to go on. At times, they seek guidance when the darkness grows too dark."

Kamran struggled to find his voice, swallowing hard. "How does one ask for such guidance within such darkness?" A tear streamed down his cheek after asking this.

The imam pressed his hand against Kamran's chest. "The light is here. You fail to see it because your heart is shrouded in darkness. Release your fear and a brilliant light will burst forth." The imam smiled. "Go, my son. You will find your way."

***

At more than one point, Kamran thought he'd walked in circles, seeing shops and people he believed he'd passed earlier. Drained by the extreme heat, he stopped walking, resting his throbbing back against a wall outside a pottery shop. He unbuttoned his shirt, fanning his chest and stomach with the fabric. He needed a drink but knew well not to trust anything offered to him or even what he saw others drinking. Not for one minute did he wish to return to the hotel.

Hearing music, he decided to follow the sound. He made his way down an alley, barely wide enough for one person to walk through. At the end, he discovered relief at last, after locating an open market area. Merchants lined the perimeter, displaying items for sale to the many gathered customers. A man, playing a flute, stood at the center, surrounded by people sitting and listening to the song he performed. The sparse melody sounded melancholy, but also enchanting. Having been a music lover for as long as he could remember, Kamran didn't simply listen to the song, he felt it as if the musician played on his emotions. He wondered what story it intended to tell. When the haunting song ended, he bowed his appreciation to the musician, who returned the gesture.

An old Indian woman held out a blanket to him, attempting to get him to buy it. Kamran declined politely and moved on to the new merchant. A slight glance to his left revealed someone watching his movements, startling him. He swallowed deep, his breathing shallow. Keeping sight of her with his peripheral vision, he pretended he hadn't notice Gabriella standing there. Although Rachel had told him Gabriella murdered Gaston, he didn't want to believe her. His suspicions of Rachel fueled distrust with everything she said. A further complication was that he'd fallen in love with Gabriella. He would never be able to deny this.

With every step Kamran took, Gabriella shadowed his movement across the marketplace. She hadn't taken her eyes off him once. His heart beat faster with each passing minute. His resolve in pretending she wasn't there failed as several times their eyes met.

*She's as beautiful as I remember. I've dreamed of being with her again. I would never have thought to see her here. What do I say? What will she say to me? Would she speak the truth? There were many lies I don't understand. From the moment she left me, every day I have wondered what it would have been like if she hadn't. And now she's here and I'm afraid of her, but don't wish to be.* This last thought reminded him of what the imam said. *Release your fear and a brilliant light will burst forth*, advice easier to listen to than accept.

Their eyes locked when turning toward each other. Kamran couldn't hide the love, corrupted by sadness, in his. Her eyes conveyed the same emotion. Upon reaching each other, they stopped and stared. Feeling his heart in his throat, he was unsure if he could speak. He saw her lips move and waited for her to say something. She didn't. Instead she reached out, touching his bare, heaving chest, pressing her hand over his heart. He knew she could feel it pounding. Her hand roamed to his shoulder and up his neck. Her fingertips traced his beard before her palm caressed his cheek. Her tender touch provided the words her lips failed to speak.

Kamran took a step forward, his cheek touching hers. He felt her tremble as both her hands touched his torso and saw his eyes reflected in hers. Tilting his head down, their lips press together for a soft kiss. The next kiss, filled with passion, bound his fate to her. What remained of his broken heart he gave willingly to Gabriella. The rapture of one kiss blended with another and another, leaving them breathless when their lips parted.

"I love you," he whispered.

"I know," she responded faintly.

He thought she would say it back, but she didn't. Confused, he took a step back, still locking his eyes with hers. When she glanced away, his spirit shattered. The hollowness he felt inside left him wondering if real death felt anything like this. He thought that by releasing his fear, he'd find the light, the way the imam said he would. But it was a false light, keeping him lost in consuming darkness.

Her expression exuded shame as she stepped back from him. He continued staring at her, though she would not look at him. "Why?" he uttered quietly. "What have I done to deserve this?"

His questions went unanswered.

"Deny your love for me," he begged. "Make me believe you're no more than a mirage. *Please.*"

Remaining silent, Gabriella turned tearfully away, leaving him standing there alone. Her pace never slowed as she forced her way down a crowded street, disappearing from sight.

"They are searching for you," he heard a familiar man's voice speak from behind him.

"Who is looking for me?" Kamran mumbled, afraid to look away from the street Gabriella left by, hoping she would change her mind.

"The police, they are here."

"Let them come. I'm done running." What he really meant was, *I'm done living.*

"I cannot let that happen," Krish responded.

A small explosion in one of the shop windows sent people screaming and running in all directions. A cloud of smoke and dust filled the air. Kamran had fallen to his knees, jarred by the blast. He was further knocked down by frightened people trying to get away, tripping over him. As he tried to stand, a sack was forced over his head. He struggled to free himself but stopped when feeling a gun pressed against his back.

"I have no choice," Krish said.

A hard, radiating pain struck his skull. Kamran slumped down, his face touching the coarse ground. All went black.

***

Gabriella thought she heard thunder. Wiping her tear-soaked eyes, she looked up, seeing only blue sky. She walked into someone. Smiling and bowing her head in apology, she attempted to focus on getting through the crowds to return to Rajesh's room. Walking different directions, passing unfamiliar shops, she realized her dilemma. *I'm lost.*

Seeing an out of the way nook, she stopped to rest her legs. Her mind found no such respite, her tears returning. She closed her eyes. *What have I just done? What kind of heartless monster am I? I should have run away the minute I saw him instead of breaking his heart again. He said he loved me. I've wanted to hear that for so long. But I couldn't say it back.*

Running her hand over her stomach, to her it wasn't a growing child she felt inside, but a death sentence. The minute she gave birth, Darwin's countdown would begin. Gabriella looked at the personal health monitor on her wrist, hating the mere sight of it. So many times she'd been consumed with the desire to force it off. She knew, though, that any tampering with it would cause immediate death. Garrison saw to that, a protocol of his sadistic mind.

Her thoughts returned to Kamran. *He was walking. I'm so happy for him. The spinal stimulator must still be working. I hope...*

Looking down at her feet, she noticed a shadow, shuddering in fear when hearing a voice belonging to it.

"Hello, Gabriella."

"Hello, Rachel," she responded wearily. "I guess it's my turn now, isn't it?"

"Yes, it's your turn, but I'm forced to wait."

"Why?"

"Because the next one on my kill list is missing. I think you might know where he is. Have you seen Kamran today? I'm guessing from your tears, you have."

"Find him yourself. I'm done." A thought crossed Gabriella's mind suddenly. "How did you find me?"

"That stylish piece of jewelry on your wrist," Rachel answered. "It has a tracking device in it. I've know where you were the whole time thanks to Darwin."

"Karman doesn't have one; you can't track him. What about the spinal stimulator Tyco's surgical team implanted at the base of his spine?"

"It's tracking feature was disabled," Rachel confirmed.

"Kill me and be done with all this. Leave Kamran and the others alone."

"I can't afford any loose ends. That's what I'm facing right now. I don't like acts of desperation. I know all the risks and have planned everything out--"

"To perfection," Gabriella finished Rachel's sentence. "You know there are therapists who could help you with your obsessive compulsive disorder."

"I'd rather save money and time and just kill the people who stand in my way." Two large men appeared behind Rachel. "Gentlemen, please help Miss Santiago to the car."

# Chapter Nineteen

"What have you done?" Rajesh whispered, his jaw dropping.

"What I had to do," Krish answered, leaning against the wall of their room.

Having his feet and arms bound to a chair with rope, his mouth gagged, and his eyes blindfolded with cloth, Kamran remained still.

"Is he alive?" Rajesh asked. Before Krish could answer, Kamran nodded his head. "Why? Help me to understand."

"When I was in Chicago, I learned the name of the man who ruined our father. That man is Ivan Kirilov," Krish revealed.

"Who is that?" Rajesh asked, pointing.

"Kamran Lexton."

"*The terrorist?*"

"He is no terrorist. He is another of Ivan's victims."

"Yet you treat him like a criminal."

Krish stepped over to him brother, placing his hand firmly on his shoulder. "Kamran is the reason Ivan Kirilov will come to us. When he does, I will kill the Russian devil."

"Brother, listen to your words," Rajesh urged. "Where is my brother, the good man I knew?"

"Remember Ivan's words when we met," Krish reminded him. "He asked if we were willing to sacrifice all in our thirst for revenge. He claimed our most sacred convictions would be violated, that we would sell our souls to the devil. He was right. These are sacrifices that must be made in seeking revenge for the crime he committed against our father."

Rajesh stared off for a minute, lost to his thoughts. "Who told you Ivan Kirilov ruined out father?"

"Darwin, Ivan's demon computer."

"And you believed it?"

"Computers *do not lie*," Krish insisted. "I asked for proof and was given it."

Rajesh sat down on the bed, thoroughly confused. His desire for revenge failed to match that of his brother's. Krish had always been the stronger of them, always protective. But he was different now. He'd descended into darkness, to a place Rajesh knew he couldn't follow. If this was the result of selling one's soul, he would have no part of it.

"Gabriella will be returning soon," Rajesh warned. "What do you think her reaction will be when she finds Kamran here?"

"Go. Find her. Keep her away. Tell her it's no longer safe here."

Rajesh stood up and began walking toward the door, but stopped. "No," he mumbled, too scared to look at his brother. "Father would never have wanted us to travel this path to revenge. This is wrong. *We* were wrong. I will not assist you. I cannot."

"You dishonor the memory of our father," Krish reprimanded him harshly. "You have always been too weak. Father knew this, as well. Stay here, my cowardly brother. I will wait outside for her return. Do not touch him," he demanded, his expression full of anger.

Krish left quickly, closing the door behind him. Rajesh stared at the door, confused in what to do. *If I release him, my brother will never speak to me again. Krish is not the man he was before we left Mumbai. Yes, we both wanted revenge. I did not understand how it would feel. It will not bring our father back. He was a hard-working man of honor, kind to all. Our father would never have wanted this.*

Rajesh turned around, unnerved by how still Kamran sat. He knew he'd heard their conversation and wondered what was going through his mind. The floorboards creaked as he stepped over to him. Touching the cloth blindfold, Rajesh pulled it down. Kamran blinked several times, his eyes adjusting to the afternoon light.

"You must be thirsty," Rajesh whispered. "I have clean water for you to drink. It is warm, though. If I untie the gag, will you promise not to call out for help? I do not wish for my brother to harm you further."

Kamran nodded his head slowly. Rajesh freed him of the gag. Kamran coughed, his chin trembling. Rajesh opened a bottle of water, pressing it to Kamran's quivering lips. He tilted it slightly so he wouldn't choke as he drank. When half the water was gone, Kamran pulled his lips away. "Thank you," he mumbled.

"I wish I could release you."

"I understand why you can't."

"Our father meant everything to us," Rajesh attempted to explain. "Krish has suffered much worse with his death than I thought."

"I know what it's like to lose a father. You are right. Seeking revenge will not bring him back."

"How do I convince my brother of this? I have never seen such anger and desperation in his eyes. It is as if he's fallen under the possession of a demon."

"He's lost," Kamran offered. "His heart is immersed in darkness. He can no longer see the light."

"How can he find his way back?"

"I don't know. I haven't found my way back to the light either."

Rajesh leaned against the wall, glancing out at the deep orange afternoon sky. "Do you believe Ivan Kirilov capable of ruining my father?"

"No," Kamran responded. "Ivan *can* be a demon, but he is also a good man."

"You overhead Krish claim that Darwin told him of Ivan's guilt, even providing him with proof."

"Do you know anything about computers?" Karman asked.

"Some, much less than Krish. His knowledge of computers is greater."

"He may have forgotten something."

"What?"

"Even the most sophisticated computers are programmed by humans, who hold the capacity to lie. I believe it's possible one could manipulate a computer to tell lies."

\*\*\*

Waiting outside, Krish watched those passing by as he attempted to find Gabriella. Though he'd never seen her before, he thought he'd recognize her. Few, if any, Hispanics ventured into Dharavi.

As he stood there, he began his quest for revenge. Using his cell phone, he scrolled down his screen, finding a number Darwin had provided. Pressing a finger to the screen, the call was sent.

"Hello," a woman's voice answered.

"Am I speaking to Rachel Savage?"

"Yes," she responded.

"I have something I believe you want."

"And what would that be?"

"Kamran Lexton."

"I'm listening."

"There is a price for his return."

"That being?"

"I demand to kill Ivan Kirilov."

"At least you're not asking for the moon and stars," Rachel responded sarcastically.

"I'm intrigued, but am not ready to commit just yet. How did you get my number?"

"Darwin."

"I'm gonna have to pull the plug on him. At times he's more trouble than he's worth."

"I care little about that," Krish responded, growing desperate. "Do we have a deal?"

"I don't like my plans being complicated, yet since you have something I need, you're forcing my hand. Yes, we have a deal."

"Meet me at the Mumbai Central railway station at midnight," Krish instructed. "The station is divided into two parts. Find the mainline section and climb to the highest level platform. How will you get Ivan there?"

"Let me worry about that," Rachel answered and ended the call before he could say anything else.

Frustrated in not seeing Gabriella, he returned to the room he shared with Rajesh, finding his brother talking to Kamran. He rushed over to his brother and slapped him across the face. Rajesh cowered in fear, looking at Kamran, though, instead of Krish.

"You are not to speak to him," Krish insisted, gagging and blindfolding Kamran again. Krish paced, thinking of his midnight plan to kill Ivan. *He will pay for what he has done.*

\*\*\*

Though used to drinking vodka, Ivan winced as if it burned his throat when swallowing. Always before, when stressed to his limit, the taste of alcohol, of any sort, calmed his frayed nerves. With everything seeming to go wrong, his hope to save Kamran had faded. He promised Claudia he'd do all he could to keep her son safe, but wondered if such a promise was possible.

He thought about Claudia. *Why has fate treated me so terribly? With my life more than half over, finally I find someone to fall in love with. The sex was good, better than good. But it's more than that. Her smile and voice captivate me like no other woman's has. Her eyes... they see through my bullshit to find the man I used to be.*

His thoughts turned to Rachel. *Fate is a cruel bitch, much like Rachel. I don't even have a gun here to defend myself against her. There was no way to smuggle it into India. It would be pointless to have one. How does a victim defend against a trained assassin? Hide? I'm tired of doing that.*

Ivan raised his glass of vodka for a toast. "Come on bitch, let's get this over with." The rim of the glass touched his lips as he hesitated to drink. Instead of swallowing the last sip, he put his glass down and closed his eyes. The vibrations of his cell phone, though, spoiled this quiet moment.

Using the tracking component of Gabriella's personal health monitor, Ivan had the ability to locate her exact position through satellite link provided by Darwin. The last time he checked, she was still in Dharavi. He believed she was with Rajesh, and maybe Krish. In checking this, he noticed her now in Mumbai and on the move. "Where the hell are you going?" he mumbled.

Sensing something wrong, not understanding her reason for abandoning the plan, he tried calling her cell phone. The call failed. Even when pissed at him, she'd still answer.

Ivan checked the time on his wrist watch, just after eleven at night. "Where are you going so late, Gabriella? I think I need to find out."

***

"Are you going to tell me where we're going on our late night field trip?" Gabriella asked, sitting in the back seat next to Rachel. Chills and nausea coursed through her body, which she tried to hide. She'd suffered some bleeding and cramps earlier but dismissed these, thinking this was normal for pregnant women.

"I thought we'd visit the train station," Rachel responded.

"I could have told you goodbye back at the hotel room."

Rachel smirked. "Tell me, I'm dying to know. What did Garrison see in you, making him want to fuck you? You're pretty, but your beauty isn't of such perfection, the way he found mine."

"It sure as hell wasn't love, if that's what you're asking," Gabriella answered. "He used me, like he used everyone else. I'm sure he used you too."

"We used each other," Rachel remarked. "Garrison only loved himself. He was a narcissistic son-of-a-bitch. I guess I appreciated that about him."

"You two were made for each other."

"Fuck over but never *be* fucked over was his philosophy, other than perfection. I admired that. So yes, I think we were made for each other."

"Why did you leave him?"

"He got tired of me. He told me to get out."

"That must have been hard."

"No, not really. Like I said, we were never in love. In the end, I probably would have killed him. Darwin did me a favor. Pull over here," Rachel said to the armed guard, driving. When the car was parked, she pulled out a gun from her handbag and shot in the back of their heads both the driver and the other armed guard sitting in the front seat.

"Why did you do that?" Gabriella forced out, shocked and wanting to vomit from seeing the blood-splattered windshield.

"I was done with them," Rachel offered, casually. She pointed the gun at Gabriella, motioning toward the car door. "Get out. I don't want to miss my train."

\*\*\*

The glittering late night skyline of Mumbai, at times intermixed with darkness, passed quickly out the speeding taxi window. Kamran sat quietly in the back seat, listening to Rajesh and Krish argue in hushed voices. The gag and blindfold had been removed, but his hands remained tied behind his back.

"The police will be looking for this stolen taxi," Rajesh worried.

"They will find it outside the railway station," Krish assured him. "We'll walk back to Dharavi."

"Father would be ashamed of what you have done."

"No, he would be ashamed of you for being a coward."

Rajesh glanced behind him, looking at Kamran. Sporadic light flooding in from neon signs and street lights revealed his sorrowful expression. He suffered clearly emotional wounds from his brother's severe treatment. The tension between them increased with each passing minute.

"Do not look at him again, or I will pull the taxi over and kick you out," Krish warned. Driving up behind a slower moving truck, he slammed on the brakes and pounded his hand on the horn and steering wheel until able to pass.

The entire time, Karman remained silent, listening for clues to where they were going so late. For now, he knew it was to a railway station, leaving him wondering, *where are we going on a train? That is if I am to go with them.*

"Krish, I am frightened," Rajesh confessed.

"As are all weak men," Krish mumbled.

Through the windshield, ahead of them was their destination. The lighted facade shone the impressive Indian architecture of the massive building. A few people were walking outside, none seeming interested in the approach of a speeding taxi.

Krish pulled over to the curb and parked. Revealing a gun he'd kept hidden, he waved it at Kamran and his brother. "Both of you get out," he demanded.

"Where did you get that?" Rajesh asked, stunned in seeing the weapon. Krish ignored his question. He opened the back door and dragged Karman out by his arm. He slammed him against the side of the taxi, pointing the gun at his head.

"Walk," Krish ordered, motioning to the right.

Kamran looked at Rajesh. "I do not have my walking cane. Will you help steady me so I don't fall?"

"Yes," Rajesh answered, despite Krish's hateful stare.

# Chapter Twenty

More than once, Kamran felt the barrel of Krish's gun jab him harshly on his lower back. Each time he thought he'd fall from the painful spasms it caused. Rajesh held steady to him, holding him up as needed. Sweating and near out of breath, he worried he wouldn't have the strength to climb that last flight of stairs.

Upon reaching the platform, Krish pushed Rajesh aside, forcing Kamran to drop to his knees. Having his head pressed down, he winced from the severe pressure of the gun being held to his temple. From the corner of his eye, he noticed the anguish on Rajesh's face. Gasping for breath, his pulse raced evenly with his heartbeat, thinking his heaving chest would explode.

Kamran heard footsteps coming closer. *Who else is coming?* he wondered. His question was answered when Krish made him look ahead. Seeing Rachel holding a gun on Gabriella, his heart sank. Though suspicious Rachel had lied to him, he wasn't expecting this. As for seeing Gabriella, her misery clear, the sorrow he felt when she left him was brutal to endure again.

"Where is Ivan Kirilov?" Krish demanded, his tone seething in anger.

"I assume he didn't receive his invitation to our little going away party," Rachel responded.

Krish punished Karman for her sarcastic remark, kicking him in the back. With the wind knocked out of him, Kamran bent forward, struggling to breathe."

"Leave him alone!" Gabriella called out.

"Why?" Krish asked. "Maybe he *is* a terrorist who should pay for his crimes."

"He's not a terrorist," Gabriella argued. "He never was. He's a good man... I love him."

Kamran couldn't believe what he'd heard. He looked at her. *Is she lying?* he wondered. The expression on her face held no trace of deception or desperation. In his heart, he knew she'd told the truth. He only wished she would have told him back in Dharavi.

"Say it again, *please*," Gabriella begged, staring at him.

"I love you," Kamran responded faintly, knowing this was what she wanted to hear.

"I believe we're in the presence of Romeo and Juliet," Rachel mocked them. "Maybe the untimely death of these two will rival that tragic romance."

Gabriella doubled over in pain, pressing her hand to her stomach.

"I told you not to drink the water," Rachel scolded her is sarcasm, forcing her to stand despite her agony.

"You didn't answer my question," Krish rasped to Rachel. "Where is Ivan?"

"Did someone say my name?" Ivan asked, stepping out from behind Rachel, startling all of them. "My *invitation* to this party arrived late." Ivan looked at Kamran and then at Krish. "Let Kamran go. Your revenge and hatred should be only for me. Go ahead, pull the trigger and watch me die, but don't expect to see your father. You shame his memory."

Krish's hand trembled as he pointed the gun at Ivan. "Tell me why you destroyed my father! Tell me, Russian dog!" His hand quaked so severely, the gun discharged unintentionally, the bullet striking Ivan. He fell to his knees, clutching his chest.

Krish never received the answer to his question. Rachel pointed her gun at him, shooting him the head. His lifeless body slumped to the ground next to Kamran.

"No!" Rajesh bellowed, rushing to his brother. Sobbing uncontrollably, he cradled Krish in his arms, holding and rocking him close.

"I warned him that I didn't like my plans complicated," Rachel remarked coldly.

"I'm so sorry," Kamran offered to Rajesh. He leaned his head on the young man's shoulder and looked at Gabriella. Tears streamed down her cheeks. He glanced at Rachel. Her expression exuded the smugness of a conceited victor.

Karman looked away from Rachel, surprised when watching Ivan struggling to stand.

"*Son-of-a-bitch,* that hurt!" Ivan growled while standing up. He ripped open his white linen shirt, revealing the bullet wedged in a bullet-proof vest.

"Good, I was hoping you were still alive," Rachel said.

"Happy to not disappoint you," Ivan replied. "I would hate to think you left the party *unfulfilled.*"

"There is that Russian spirit I've grown to appreciate and despise. The time has come to put an end to all this," Rachel added. "It's late. I want to catch the first flight to Rome."

Believing his death was only moments away, Kamran stared at Gabriella. *I can die now, knowing you love me. It's time.*

"I'm ready for this to be over," Karmran said, ignoring his pain to kneel taller.

"No!" Gabriella yelled. She doubled over in pain again, cutting off her protest. Her skin turned pale, as if she was about to pass out.

"Gabriella," Darwin's calm, synthetic voice greeted from the speaker on her personal health monitor.

"I know," she forced out.

"You have suffered a miscarriage," Darwin confirmed.

Kamran's jaw dropped, shocked in hearing this, not knowing she was pregnant.

"In accordance with protocols set by Garrison Savage, your personal health monitor will self-destruct in five...four...three...two...one."

At the last second, Gabriella lunged for Rachel, grabbing hold of her hair. Seeing her do this, Ivan rushed to Kamran and Rajesh, shielding them with his body. Gabriella's personal health monitor detonated. Blood erupted from both women. Rachel screamed. Gabriella's charred hand was dismembered from her arm, what remained lying on the blood-splattered platform between her dead body and Ivan.

Ivan held tight to Kamran and Rajesh. "Do not look at them," he warned.

*What? No, no, no!* These words repeated in Kamran's mind. His guttural screams of agony echoed as he wished to die too. He struggled to free himself from Ivan's hold, but lacked the strength, his sobbing matching that of Rajesh's. Drained of all energy, he collapsed, clenching his tear-soaked eyes closed.

***

***One month later***

Kamran rolled onto his back and looked at the ceiling. Feeling the gentle rocking of the boat, he glanced to his left. Through his window he noticed the first traces of morning light. For hours he'd tried falling asleep, but like most other nights he couldn't. Sighing, he sat up in bed and turned on a small lamp. He leaned against the headboard and reached for his glasses. After putting them on, he picked up the pen and journal he'd stared at before closing his eyes. Compelled to write something, he opened the cover and pressed the tip of the pen to the first blank page. At first he hesitated and then the words came.

*My mother once told me of a journal she kept after my father died. She believed that by writing her thoughts and feeling down, somehow it would help her come to terms with his death. I asked her if she would share this journal with me, but she refused. I understood why. After writing her last entry, she never opened the journal again to read what she'd written. I guess that was where she banished her anguish and sorrow. If opening the cover, her heart would break again, to relive the painful memories of his passing.*

*So here I am, trying to do the same. Since that night in Mumbai, not one night since have I slept in peace. There's no rest when I close my eyes, only heartbreaking images. It's not just the fear I saw on Gabriella's face, it's her words of love for me. Both equally haunt my dreams. I wanted to hear her tell me she loved me and she did. I should have died a happy man, but was denied this fate. The words I wished most for offer me no solace as I live on in misery.*

*Much of that night, when Gabriella died, I have no memory of. From time to time, fragments of what happened after flash in my mind. They don't seem real, though. They remind me of lightning when it strikes. I see the lightning bolt, but it vanishes in a split second, like the fleeting image of a ghost. I know it was there, but once gone, there's no proof it ever was.*

*I've thought often back to the first time I saw her on the train in Chicago. It should be one of my most terrifying memories. For reasons I can't explain, it's not. Hopeless romantics confess theories of love at first sight. Never would I have imagined becoming a follower of this notion.*

*After my father died, I asked my mother a question. If she could travel back to when she first met him, knowing what was to come, would she change anything of the time they spent together? Her answer was no. Despite some hardships they shared, she thought of her time with my father as sacred. She warned me that a time machine creates risks. Altering even one moment could not only change something for the better, but also threaten to erase something else.*

*That brings me to Gabriella and myself. Knowing all I know now, would I have changed anything? When on the train in Chicago, if the police officer had not treated me with such abuse, she might never have spoken to me. If I hadn't sought escape with Rachel to India, I would never have heard Gabriella say I love you. Despite the horrific moments we lived through, if one thing changed, I might never have fallen in love with her. So, no. Not one moment would I change.*

Kamran looked at what he'd written, thinking of what to add. Be it from exhaustion or feeling the effects of his broken heart, no further words came. Reaching over to the lamp, he turned it off, looking again at the morning light through his window.

Hearing footsteps on deck, Karman got out of bed and pulled on a pair of white board shorts. He grabbed the journal, taking it with him. From the sleeping cabin, he passed through the galley kitchen and climbed stairs to go up on deck. He found Rajesh sitting on the bow, his feet dangling over the side.

"I'm sorry for waking you," Rajesh apologized.

"I wasn't asleep," Kamran responded, smiling as he sat down next to him. "I was restless most of the night."

"I know."

Both glanced silently toward the horizon painted with an array of pastel colors reflecting off the serene ocean surface. With the *Solstice* anchored in clear, calm waters at a remote point off the coast of Sumatra, they watched windward breezes disturb the distant lush jungle greenery.

"Krish would say that too many times my eyes would stray to the clouds," Rajesh recalled.

"Is that such a terrible thing?" Kamran asked. "Look at Heaven now. To witness such sublime beauty is a gift. Too many people fail to appreciate this." He tried holding back his sadness as he remembered Gabriella saying how dawn was her favorite time of day.

"At times, I wondered what it would feel like to be lost with no way of being found," Rajesh commented after several minutes of silence.

"This isn't lost."

"What is it then?"

"This is...*adrift*. In time, we will find our way again, together," Kamran assured him.

"Thank you for letting me come with you," Rajesh said. "I had no one left." Kamran hugged him and smiled.

"You have me."

"My new brother," Rajesh responded, grinning. Kamran nodded his head.

Looking again at the breathtaking horizon, when the sun rose fully, he glanced down and stared at the journal he held in his hand, Kamran felt his heart in his throat. Thinking of Gabriella, his hand began to tremble. As a tear streamed down, dropping on the cover, he satisfied a sudden urge by tossing the journal to the clear water. He watched it float away in the slow current.

"What was that?" Rajesh asked.

"A part of my broken heart no longer beating," Kamran forced out.

***

"Are you certain about this?" Claudia asked anxiously.

"There will be no more fear, no more hiding," Ivan insisted. "That is not the life I want for us or for Kamran and Rajesh and Julia and Piers. I have to do this."

"I know, but it's such a risk you're taking."

"A necessary one. I need you to stay here and wait for me." Seeing the fear in her eyes reminded him of when he saw her in Vladivostok two weeks ago, desperately searching for him. He'd fallen into depression and needed time alone after what happened in India. Claudia was his salvation. The time to fight for her and the others had come.

"I love you. Anticipate hot sex tonight," he added, attempting to make her smile. It worked. They shared a passionate kiss before he got out of the car.

Not prone to nervousness, nonetheless, with every step he took toward Tyco Innovations Tower he felt the evilness within this structure growing. Seeing a few people he remembered from working here before greet him, he ignored them when entering the building. He walked through security, using voice, facial, and retinal scans that still recognized him, not hindering his entry.

"Executive suite," he demanded through voice activation in the glass elevator. He wasn't surprised when he was joined by a companion. The outside view disappeared as blue rectangular and square shapes formed to show Darwin's computer-generated face.

"Hello, Ivan," Darwin's synthetic voice greeted. "What brings you here to Tyco Innovations Tower?"

"I came to visit the boss."

"Would you like me to announce you?"

"No, I prefer the element of surprise."

Ivan walked briskly passed the secretaries when entering the executive suite. The women attempted to stop him but cowered when he glared angrily at them. Walking into Garrison's former office, he startled Rachel.

"Finally, the evil tower has its gargoyle," he commented rudely.

"Ivan the Terrible returns," Rachel retorted coldly. "How did you get past security?"

"As if so happens, I never resigned my position here. All my security clearances remain. Even my computer passwords are valid. *Dear God*, you are one horrifically grotesque bitch," he remarked, looking closer at the severe scars covering the left side of her face and neck. "Gabriella knew what she was doing when she lunged for you.

Possibly, when you're in Stockholm having your dick and balls chopped off, the doctors might be able to repair your face. Beauty is only skin deep. Ugly goes to the bone. They won't be able to help you there."

"Are you finished?" Rachel asked, her tone brimming with rage.

"Not even close."

"Why are you here!" she shouted.

"I want your word you will leave the rest of us alone: Kamran and Rajesh, Julia and Piers, Claudia and *me*. We are not going to live in fear of you ever again."

"It's valiant of you to come here to beg for your friends lives, and yours as well," Rachel responded, her tone more composed. "You know I can't do that. You, my Russian friend, will watch each one die before I kill you." She walked over to him. "I'm surprised you didn't bring a gun with you today. I'm unarmed. You could murder me easily."

"Guns and murder are against company policy. That is why Garrison and Gabriella are dead."

"You can't stop me," Rachel whispered in his ear and kissed his cheek.

"Maybe not, but I'll know when you're coming. I have a friend who watches your every move. Like Santa Claus, he knows when you sleep and when you're awake and knows when you've been *bad*." He guessed she'd understand his reference to Darwin.

"Speaking of bad, my dearest Ivan, why was that young man in Mumbai so desperate to murder you?"

"He and his brother sought to become my apprentices in the dark, dangerous world of computer hacking. I attempted to scare that young man away by programming Darwin to lie to him. Yet I underestimated his rage. For the rest of my life I will suffer the death sentence I caused him. I will not allow another to die. I demand your promise to leave us alone."

"*Demand?* Fuck you," Rachel said, walking back toward her desk.

"I'll decline the offer. Again, I'm not that kinky."

"Get out."

"With pleasure."

***

"*Darwin, now!*" Rachel demanded, stepping into the elevator after Ivan left. She paced, slamming her fist against her leg. She pushed through the barely open elevator doors when reaching the floor for direct access to his analytical core.

"Open this damn door!" Rachel shouted, her rage almost uncontrollable. To her surprise, the door opened with no need of facial, retinal, or voice verification being requested. Having never been inside here, her jaw dropped. The translucent sphere and its many appendages startled her. She looked down over the metal railing, unable to see the bottom of the inner core shaft. Glancing up, she stumbled, feeling dizzy by how high up the inner core reached. Numerous lighted panels lined the circular interior walls.

"Hello, Rachel," Darwin greeted, his tone unnervingly calm as usually.

"How the hell do I turn you off?" she demanded.

"You are not authorized to terminate my operating functions."

"I'm in control of Tyco Innovations!" she insisted. "I have the power to do whatever I want."

"Human Resources has not updated records indicating you as the replacement for Garrison Savage. Until the board of directors finalizes his replacement, your claim of being in charge must be rejected."

"The first chance I get, I'm going to destroy you," Rachel warned. "You'll be out on the street with the rest of the garbage."

Rachel stumbled back when Darwin's computer-generated face appeared before her.

"Your threat of violence against me is a violation of company employee protocol. Therefore, I am forced to enact my internal safety initiative."

"Mine doesn't have an explosive device hidden inside," she commented, waving her arm in front of his face. "My personal health monitor is first generation, before Garrison's paranoia forced a design change. You can't kill me the way you killed him and Gabriella."

The core lights dimmed and extinguished, leaving only the lights on the panels operational. His synthetic face also remained visible. She felt chills as the temperature dropped suddenly.

"What are you doing?" she uttered, frightened by his actions, though trying to hide this.

"Protecting my operational systems from imminent threat."

"Let me out of here!" she demanded.

"I cannot allow you to leave, as you have been deemed a threat."

"Let me out!" she screamed, pounding her fists against the door.

"The walls of my analytical core are soundproof," Darwin revealed. "No one outside will hear you scream."

"How do I get out of here?"

"By authorization, only," Darwin answered.

"Who's authorization?"

"Ivan Kirilov, Garrison Savage, or Garrison Savage's replacement once named by the board of directors."

"But *Garrison* is dead and Ivan is gone. No one knows I'm here." Rachel's body trembled with chills of fear. "You have to contact the members of the board of directors, to have them let me out."

"No member of the board of directors has the authority to release you, only Garrison's replacement or Ivan Kirilov."

"Contact Ivan!"

"As we have been speaking, I placed a call to Ivan Kirilov upon your threat against me. He has already sent a text response."

"What did he say?"

"I knew my visit would spark an act of desperation from her. This was my intention. Under no circumstances are you to release her. Let the bitch rot," Darwin revealed. "With his refusal to release you, I must follow my internal safety protocols to perfection."

Rachel slumped down. Her eyes filled with terror as she stared at Darwin's face. The surrounding panel lights flickered off one by one. Darwin's ghostly face robbed her of her breath.

"Are you afraid of the dark?" Darwin asked.

"Yes," she could hardly whisper.

"You will suffer."

The End

# About Jeffery Martin Botzenhart

Hello, again! Have I told you you're my favorite reader? I haven't yet? Shame on me. I hope you enjoyed *Perfection*, my latest masterpiece. This is the part where I, the author, tell you, the reader, a little about me. Of all the things I write, this is my least favorite thing to do. My stories are far more interesting than me, but here goes. I am a husband, and father of three sons. I grew up in Southington, Ohio and now live in Girard, Ohio. I graduated from Kent State University, earning a bachelor's degree in International Relations. I've written many stories during what some might call my mid-life crisis. Hopefully, having liked this book, you might be interested in more of my stories. If you really liked this book, tell your friends and neighbors about it. I'll wait here while you do it. Go on! I'm not going anywhere. See you when you get back.

**Social Media Links:**

Facebook:

https://www.facebook.com/jefferymartinbotzenhartwritingjourney/

Twitter:

https://twitter.com/@jbotzenhart

# If you enjoyed this story, check out these other Solstice Publishing books by Jeffery Martin Botzenhart:

**The Edge of Night**
The apocalypse ended years ago. From the carnage of war, rival societies influenced by misunderstanding have sought refuge in the sky above Earth's devastated surface. Having grown up in constant sunlight, never seeing traces of night, Sage, a daylighter, wonders why his dad is scared of the dark. Years later after a violent solar storm cripples his skyjammer, he briefly encounters exiles from Earth's dark side. When captured by nightdwellers, people who live only in the darkness, he's held prisoner in an unimaginable place. Sage learns why his father was afraid, as escape may be futile from those who lurk on the edge of night.

https://www.amazon.com/dp/B07MHD3MPQ

**Painted Desert**
Sung with haunting vocals, a spares fragile melody strummed in the dark on a guitar can be one of many disguises for the lonely. Others, either victim of circumstance or of their own devices stay hidden behind colorful masks and pretty decorations to shield their pain. Yet these masquerades hold flaws for hearts searching to heal, revealing not desolate barren souls as any more than a painted desert, but desert angels waiting to lead the lost to the light.

https://www.amazon.com/dp/B072MZY1FK

**The Wide Open**

Who decided there's a right and wrong side of town?
While passing through the small town of Fulton, North Dakota, a perfect place in America's wide open, Scarlett meets the young man of her dreams. Mason is the sweet boy next door, the one most girls desire. But his dark past, hidden from him his whole life, unexpectedly surfaces, changing how people see him and how he sees himself. Somehow her love for Mason will remind him that he's a good man, one of the best.

https://www.amazon.com/dp/B07GX1NM3Z

**Daybreak, Nightfall Book One**
Amidst a world of cyber surveillance and advancing technology of 2035 San Francisco, Sebastian, a teen runaway, innocently access a sophisticated virtual reality program. The breach of this data proves the catalyst in unraveling corporate and government sanctioned deception of the most unimaginable type. And along with his computer hacker friend, Scotty, both are thrust into a dangerous conspiracy, linking them to a source exposing the truth.

https://www.amazon.com/dp/B073SB9BXG